P9-EKX-164

A Melanie Kroupa Book

CONFESS-O-RAMA

RON KOERTGE

Orchard Books
New York

Orchard Books
95 Madison Avenue
New York, NY 10016

Manufactured in the United States of America
Book design by Chris Hammill Paul

10 9 8 7 6 5 4 3 2

The text of this book is set in 12 point Bembo.

Library of Congress Cataloging-in-Publication Data

Koertge, Ronald.
    Confess-O-Rama / Ron Koertge.
        p.   cm.
    "A Melanie Kroupa book"—Half t.p.
    Summary: While his mother grieves the death of her
fourth husband, Tony vents his feelings to the Confess-
O-Rama, never suspecting who's on the other end of the
line.
    ISBN 0-531-09515-0. — ISBN 0-531-08865-0
(lib. bdg.)
    [1. Mothers and sons—Fiction. 2. Interpersonal
relations—Fiction. 3. High schools—Fiction.
4. Schools—Fiction.]   I. Title.
PZ7.K81825Co   1996
[Fic]—dc20   96-5748

For Bianca

and for Linden Ontjes,
who showed me around

took the bus to the mall. At least Mom didn't strap me in like I was the only heir to the throne and drive me herself. She'd never let me use the car because she's afraid that something might happen to me, something like . . . Wait, I can't start listing things because they go from *A* to *Z*: *avalanche–zebra stampede.*

Anyhow, when the bus driver turned to me and said, "This is it, pal," I got off and looked around.

There were kids all over the place. The little ones were walking in with their moms, and all the moms had their eyes locked onto the BACK TO SCHOOL banners like they said Hold on for Another Few Days!

Right inside the big front door, I had what my mom would call a bad moment because Bill, my stepfather, came out of a shoe store, stopped, and looked right at me. But of course it wasn't Bill. It couldn't have been Bill.

Then when I was walking past Worn Out West, there was a guy who was trying on cowboy boots like the ones my stepfather Russ used to wear. Next I saw a mannequin standing in the window of All Outdoors with the kind of waders and goofy hat that my stepfather Dennis liked. And if that wasn't enough, some guy in a tuxedo was handing out coupons. In just about every picture Mom had of my father—my real father—he was wearing a tux, because he'd been the Panamanian ambassador. Man—this wasn't a mall; it was a family album!

I bought a Coke, sat down, and took a couple of deep breaths. Lots of men walked by, men who didn't look like one of my mother's dead husbands: a mall cop, all in blue. A baker with flour on his pants. A regulation dad holding hands with both kids. That was more like it. I would just do my errands and get out of here.

All I wanted was a few school clothes. A big You Are Here map showed The Outpost just down and to the right.

On my way, I checked out the window of a store called You-Neek, where some mannequin was wearing a short black jacket, tight black pants, and silver shoes.

Maybe some kid who'd lived here a long time could get away with that, you know? Some kid who everybody knew and already liked. He could show up looking like a waiter from Saturn, and people would laugh and give him a hard time, but in a nice way. Or some girl might think he actually looked pretty cool, because there's no telling who girls will like or why. But no way I could pull that off as the new kid. Not that I wanted to. It wasn't my style. My style, if I had one, was on hold. Again.

The Outpost turned out to have a sod roof made by Plastico. Rough-hewn beams that weighed about an ounce. Salesgirls dressed in enough calico to start their own Nashville channel.

I walked up to a clerk wearing a granny bonnet, pinafore, and Converse high-tops.

"So," I asked, sounding as casual as I could, "does everybody around here wear stuff like this to school?"

Her eyes roamed the walls where a lot of stiff pants spelled out the word *PANTS*. "Pretty much. Why?"

I looked down at the scuffed floor. "Well, I just kind of moved here, but I don't want to look like I just moved here."

She put down the flannel shirts she'd been stacking and checked me out. "You look okay." She read the words SKINNY PUPPY on my shirt. "Like you're in a band or something. Your hair's cool."

I frowned. "But what does the average kid wear?"

"T-shirt. Jeans. You know."

"Not cords or khakis?"

"Cords maybe. Like in November or something. But no khakis unless you've got three or four buddies and a spray can, if you know what I mean."

"Does anybody rip their jeans at the knees and stuff?"

"Rockers, maybe. Wannabee rockers."

"Okay. Thanks. I'll, uh, you know, get some . . ."

"Clothes?"

"Yeah, right."

There were more white T-shirts than anything else, so I took some of those, plus a couple of pairs of Levi's—not too tight, not too loose.

The salesgirl was waiting for me behind the counter. I pointed. "And some of those white socks."

She looked down at my choices. "You're not like some undercover narc or anything, are you?"

"What? No!"

A crowd somewhere in the mall broke into applause. We looked toward the big double doors.

"You should go catch some of Larry's show," she said.

"Who's Larry?"

3

"Larry Deluxe from KGAB. He's like talk radio for the Valley. He's remote today from here doing School Uniforms: Pro or Con. Last year he did Available Birth Control: Pro or Con. Next year it'll be something else, pro or con."

Next year. Where would I be next year?

"Hey! Here's your change."

"Oh, yeah. Thanks." I grabbed my plastic bag, nodded good-bye.

Outside, I found another map, then took the escalator upstairs where I signed in at the Hair Affair. The receptionist wrote down my name and handed me their hair album, as big as a yearbook.

Each cut had a number by it, like a menu in a Chinese restaurant. A lot of the styles looked like auto parts—a fender here, hood ornament there. All the models looked really serious, staring off the edge of the album into the void. *I've just had my hair cut*, they seemed to say, *and it's made me reflect on my mortality.*

"Tony?"

I jumped. "That's me."

"I'm Debbie. What can I do for you today?"

Debbie's hair was red on one side, green on the other. Like a Christmas ornament.

As she tucked a white cloth around my neck I asked, "Uh, do you get a lot of kids in here? I mean, like from the high schools?"

"Pretty many." Then her hands disappeared into my hair. She lifted it up and let it sift through her fingers. She pulled it back into a short ponytail. She toyed with the front.

"Well, what's the most popular style?"

She shrugged. "Gothics want a bowl cut, jocks want a buzz, preppies like—"

"But the average kid. What does he want?"

4

"Just a haircut, I guess."

"Okay. Give me one of those."

Debbie took a look at me from three sides, squinting and twisting her mouth around. "Not too long and not too short," she said.

"Exactly."

∿∿∿∿

When I came in the front door of the condo my aunt had loaned us, I worked up a smile for my mom sitting on the green couch sorting books: *The Process of Grieving* went on one pile, *The Grief Process* on another; *You & Your Grief* floated left; *Your Grief & You* angled right.

She looked a little spaced, so I went over and took both her hands. I nodded toward the TV, which was playing with the sound off.

"See that ad for Toyotas? How many people in that red car?"

"I'm not that bad," she assured me. "But thanks."

I searched her sleepy-looking eyes. "Really?"

"Really. I'm just . . . I'm just thinking about this task here, that's all."

I glanced at the two stacks and pointed to a cheery-looking author on the dust jacket. "What's the difference?"

"Those I'm giving away to some library. The others are for you. I want you to read them, and I want you to do the exercises."

"Sure."

"Don't say it like that now. Say it like you mean it. I'm not the only one with what my many therapists called 'stuff.'"

"Please. No technical jargon."

"Promise me you'll look at them."

"I promise."

5

"Good. I know you don't like therapists, but . . ."

"The one in St. Louis wanted me to draw my anger, so I did, and she said it looked like a horsie."

"You remember that?"

I worked up a grin. "Scarred me for life."

When I walked into the kitchen and started looking through the fridge, Mom followed me. "Well, I didn't like her, either."

"How about the one in Tucson who kept calling me 'Pardner' and telling me to bite the bullet."

"We only went once."

"And then he actually handed me a bullet."

"I heard he was unorthodox, so—"

"And the two-for-one therapists in Daly City who bickered the whole session?"

"Okay, okay." She pointed to the stacks of books. "That's why I read all these. And those four over there in Tony's own personal mini-library are the best of the lot."

"I don't need any books, Mom. I'm okay. Really."

"I know. You're always okay. That's what's so scary." She put her arms around me. "I may have lost four husbands, but you lost four fathers. And all that has to come out somehow."

I stepped away, giving both her hands a squeeze as they slid off my shoulders. "I'm fine."

"You *act* fine."

I reached for one of the books in my pile. "Look. I'm holding it. Next thing you know I'll be reading it and crying in my chicken cacciatore."

"You can't hide behind that sense of humor forever. Just read the book. One thing I know," Mom said. "I'm not going to need them again. No way. I'm not putting myself through this one more time." As I opened the refrigerator door, she added, "Or you, either."

6

I just stood there, a bagel in each hand, like the hero of *Showdown at the O.K. Bakery.* "Maybe wait and see, Mom."

"Nothing to wait and see about. I'm like the albatross in that old poem; I'm bad luck."

"You're not, either. You *had* some bad luck. It's different."

"Whatever. Not that it was all bad; they were wonderful husbands and wonderful fathers. Just look how you turned out—you're a terrific kid."

"Oh, sure." I put the bagels in the microwave and punched in thirty seconds.

"You are," she assured me. "You're sweet, you're gentle, you're . . ."

"Great, I sound like one of Bambi's friends." Then I held up two covered dishes. "Turkey or tuna."

"I'm not hungry, sweetie."

I wasn't hungry, either. But if I didn't eat, she didn't eat. "Turkey," I said, sounding firm.

We sat side by side at the counter. I could see my Calphalon skillets and copper-bottomed saucepans, the ones I scrubbed so they always looked new.

She stared at her bagel suspiciously. "Did you buy these at the supermarket?"

"Mom, we're barely unpacked, and I start school tomorrow. Who has time to hunt down a real deli?"

"Speaking of school—isn't it a little odd to start on a Friday?"

I shrugged. "It's probably just find-your-room, get-your-books day."

She chewed deliberately, glancing at her reflection in the side of the toaster. "Do you think I'm getting gray?"

"All over?"

She nudged me. "My hair."

"No."

"Hmm." She opened up her sandwich and inspected it. "How was the mall? What did you buy?"

"Just, you know, school stuff."

"You got your hair cut. God, you look so much like your father sometimes." She reached over and took my hand. "Do you miss him?"

"Mom, we've been through this. I was four when he died. I don't remember very much."

"You sound cranky."

"I've been sitting on a hard bench waiting for buses. You'd be cranky, too."

She looked down at her spotless sweats, as white as the paper in my new notebooks. "I know that learner's permit is burning a hole in your pocket, but I worry about you." Her eyes started to glisten. "You're all I've got."

I wanted to avoid tears at all costs. One or two of those little guys could be like the spring thaws that start with a single drooling icicle and end up sweeping away most of St. Louis.

"Forget driving. It's okay. Don't worry about me. And I'm not cranky. I'm just hungry." I took a big bite of the sandwich I didn't want.

"One more thing, Tony."

"It's not about driving, is it?"

"No. It's about school tomorrow and West Paradise and this condo."

I waited. "Yeah?"

"We're only here till Christmas."

"I know that."

"By then all this probate stuff will be settled—the joint tenancies, the confirmation on the sale of the real properties, the—"

"Mom, I know all this. You explained it."

"I don't like it, either, Tony."

"I didn't say I didn't like it."

"But I just couldn't sit up there in Daly City and watch those real estate people walk through my memories one more time. So when your aunt Polly offered us this condo rent free . . ."

"Mom!" I waved my hand in front of her eyes. "It's okay. I'll be okay. I know how to do this."

〜〜〜〜

Next morning I just lay there: another new bed, another new place. There was only a crack or two in the ceiling, but the room looked like it'd been hit by an earthquake: stuff in boxes, boxes on their sides, a sheet tacked up to make a curtain. I'd decided to leave things the way they were. The next few months were going to be like camping out somewhere I didn't want to be, with people I wouldn't get to know.

I took a shower, shaved just to be on the safe side, slipped into my new clothes, and went downstairs. Mom was sitting at the kitchen table, drinking coffee. On the cup were the words BE SURE GET INSURED. Then Bill's phone number. Or what used to be his phone number.

I walked over. One hand came up. She gave me a long dry kiss on the cheek.

"You look nice," she said automatically.

"Really?"

She sighed and opened her eyes. "My God. Why are you dressed like a paperboy?"

"I asked the salesgirl at the mall what everybody was wearing. She said this."

Mom sat up straighter. "Well, I went to the market this

morning." She said it like kids do who've just learned to tie their own shoelaces.

"Good for you. What'd you buy?"

"Nothing. I just went."

"Not ready for the emotional commitment of standing in a line?"

"I knew I should go out. I woke up depressed, and all the experts say that the worst thing is to just hang around the house in your nightgown."

"God, you could write your own book, couldn't you. Maybe a slim volume called *Speed Grieving*. Anger and denial followed by a light lunch; then bargaining, a snack of crackers or fruit, depression, acceptance, and home by five."

She didn't smile, so I rubbed my hands together and looked toward the kitchen. There, anyway, everything was in order: my knives in their block, my spices in their rack, the fruit I'd bought in the wire basket, vegetables in the crisper.

I reached for a copper-bottomed saucepan. "How does oatmeal sound?"

No response. She was drifting again.

"I could make *huevos rancheros*."

She ran one finger over her cup and the words BE SURE. "I liked being in the market this morning."

"Good."

"I liked seeing all those single people. I thought, If they can do it, I can do it."

"Tony to Mom. Come in, Mom: eggs or oatmeal?"

"I saw a young woman with a T-shirt that said A Woman Without a Man Is Like a Fish Without a Bicycle."

"Oatmeal it is."

"I didn't understand that."

I put water on to boil, got the oatmeal jar down, and scooped out a handful. I loved the way it felt. Sure, I know

10

that oats look dry and blah, but they've got a texture all their own. They were pretty in their sea green canister: a core sample from the world of grains. And I liked their potential—a little heat, a little water, a little attention and, *violà*, a meal.

While I stirred and put an English muffin in the toaster, I kept one eye on my mother. She was pretty, the way mermaids are supposed to be pretty: slender with pale hair and skin. Thin arms, long fingers. Blue eyes, like my Levi's, bleached out a little.

I spooned hot cereal into two bowls, trickled on some of the maple syrup I'd ordered from Vermont, and set those and both halves on the counter. She took two quick bites.

"Do you like West Paradise?" she asked.

I put orange marmalade on her half of the muffin. "It's okay, I guess. Kind of a dumb name."

"You're upset with this new arrangement, aren't you."

I put my spoon down with a clunk. "No. Really."

She looked at the refrigerator. "I should have made you a lunch."

"Then you wouldn't have a son anymore, just a meal."

"Ah, but a lunch wouldn't bug me about learner's permits."

I gave her one of those twisty-mouthed smirks that meant, Very funny, then concentrated on my breakfast.

A few minutes later, I angled toward the sink, rinsed my bowl, then opened the refrigerator. "Look." I pointed. "See that blue Tupperware bowl? That's chicken salad. It's already on a bed of lettuce, just like you like it. Promise me you'll eat."

"I'll eat. And you don't have to cook for me anymore. I'm fine now. Really."

"And don't just throw that chicken salad away. I find things when you throw them away."

11

"I won't throw it away." Then when I tucked a couple of ballpoint pens in my pocket she asked, "Are you leaving?"

"Hey. I'm not shipping out with the troops. I'm just going to school."

She walked beside me toward the door. "I heard on TV that if a car is coming toward you with its lights off and you blink yours to signal the driver, he might shoot you."

I stared at her. "What are you talking about?"

"Just what I said. It's some kind of gang thing."

"You won't even let me drive. How am I going to get shot?"

She studied her white Nikes. "Remember how Dennis used to read the Bible? He had one at home, one in the pickup, and one in the *Mississippi Belle*."

"Mom?" I waved one hand in front of her eyes. "Where did Dennis come from? Bill is the grievee here, okay? Not Dennis. Dennis is history."

"The way you were standing reminded me of Dennis."

"I'll be home right after school."

"Well, be careful."

Half a block away, I slowed down, took a Walkman out of my book bag, shuffled through some cassettes, and slipped in Neil Young, turning it down low. Maybe Mom got to make every other choice, but at least I could pick any music I wanted.

West Paradise looked totally unreal to me on that first day of school. Probably the chamber of commerce had requisitioned a breeze, so all the little banners advertising a street fair stood straight out and made that canvasy snapping sound.

Robins the size of chickens traded choruses with bluebirds. Squirrels chased one another up and down trees, then sat up and looked cute. I was sure the mayor had thrown a switch for still another spectacular sunrise and was probably cueing

Snow White to come out from behind one of those older-than-God elm trees to try and sell me a souvenir sweatshirt.

As I passed some antiques stores with all that expensive old stuff, more and more kids appeared. They were on bikes and skateboards and roller blades, alone or in twos and threes. They slipped into the main stream and made a river that rolled through the suburban streets. We swept by tidy-looking houses, lots of them with those dark wood shingles. All the lawns were neat, the grass even as military school haircuts. None of the driveways had any oil spots on them. The cars were washed, and the hubcaps gleamed.

A lady in a denim shirt, Japanese gardener pants, and goat-skin gloves was on her knees in front of a perfect shrub. I watched her knock some yellow plants out of their little plastic pots and stick them in the ground. Me, too, I thought. I've just been transplanted, too.

At the corner, I turned off my music and waited at a light with five or six other kids. Two of the girls had obviously called each other up; both wore T-shirts, ripped shorts, and beat-up boots. But their hair and their makeup were perfect. If they'd been hiking, it was around a department store.

"You look nice," said A.

B. replied, "You, too."

I glanced over, but they weren't kidding, and when B. smiled at me, I looked away. I planned to keep things simple. Uncomplicated. And girls were never uncomplicated.

So I just checked out the telephone pole—reading fliers for yard sales, lost dogs, weight loss, and something called Confess-O-Rama.

Just then the light changed. On my way across the street, different car radios told me that the Dodgers had lost by two, the Clippers by twenty. A weatherman insisted that it was

13

beautiful and somebody from a talk show bellowed, "If you've been married four times or more, call me at KGAB."

Mom qualified for that. Also widowed four times. Also moved four times.

I kept up with the pack, not breaking away, not dropping back. I fiddled with the dials on my Walkman; I adjusted my book bag. Finally the north wall of the high school loomed. Underneath the arching letters *W.P.H.S.* was a huge mural. Earnest teachers lectured interested students, all seated in the grass at their feet. Paul Bunyan's sons planted a tree while a black girl and a white girl painted a scroll together.

Fifty or more of us waited at the crosswalk while a green Vette rumbled by. Beside me, taped to the side of a big electrical box, was another Confess-O-Rama flier:

Why hold it all in?
Confession's good for the soul. Call and spill your guts
to a sympathetic machine. No names, no taboos.
Anonymity guaranteed. So tell me everything!

At the bottom, like fringe on a cowgirl's skirt, hung two dozen copies of a phone number.

A hand reached past me and tore one off, so I took one, too, and tucked it away as I was nudged off the curb by the mob behind me.

I knew my homeroom was in the Art Building, so I started to search for it. The school looked like it'd been built in pieces. No big building, just a lot of low-looking greenish structures—the kind where the government stores nuclear waste.

At first the kids didn't look all that different from the ones at Daly City High: lots of girls guzzling bottled water like it was hard work pulling on those black tights, guys in black jeans and denim shirts, a Goodwill dress here, baggy sweater

14

there, some tank tops, T-shirts, khakis, cords, cutoffs, Vans. A few of the juniors and seniors sported the kind of beard that made them look like they'd spent a few days on a raft. But it must have been a chartered one, because when I took another look, everybody was a little more polished than I was used to.

Sure, one girl wore a Motley Crüe sweatshirt, but it was so clean she probably kept it in a safe. No Sonic Youth T-shirts, no Motorhead or Suicidal Tendencies. None of these kids would be mumbling along with "Fade to Black."

There were a lot of other guys dressed like me, but they were dressed better: Guess jeans, pressed T-shirts. So I fit in, but I didn't fit in. Not if you looked close.

Then I spotted the Art Building. Its windows had frosted glass, like the passion of the student Picassos had steamed it up permanently. I started that way, and almost bumped into a girl in high-topped Keds and overalls.

"My name's Rochelle." She pointed to a unicorn-shaped name tag. "What's yours."

"Uh, Tony." I looked at her red face. "Are you okay? Do you need a drink of water?

"I'm just hot." She went from tomato red to fiery red. "I mean not hot like in . . . hot. But like in temperature. You know?"

"Sure."

"We're Kids for Chastity, Tony." She pointed to two other girls, both of them with Worth Waiting For T-shirts over their baggy jeans. "And the first meeting of the semester is after school Monday." She blotted her forehead with a forearm. "We don't have any boys yet. If you joined, maybe some others would."

"I gotta go home right after school. Really."

"We could meet on Tuesday instead."

"I gotta go home every day."

"Hey! Hey, new boy! Check this out."

I turned toward a girl in a black dress, narrow as licorice, fastened with padlocks instead of buttons. She'd wrapped a long chain around her. That pulled up her dress, and everybody could see a couple of very skinny calves and a matching set of bruised-looking knees. She also carried a sign:

No Self-Control   No Restraint
No Meetings   No Vows
Instant Chastity
$19.95

"Our program is free!" said Rochelle, staring at her.

"But mine works." The skinny girl rattled the locks on her dress.

As other kids started to giggle, I began to edge away from both of them.

"Don't let her chase you away!" insisted Rochelle.

"Don't let *her* chase you away," said the other girl.

I was backpedaling like a guy on a unicycle when I tripped. My book bag went flying.

Someone boomed, "Hey, where did you think you were goin'?"

His voice cut through the chatter of the other kids, who quieted down like chimps and macaws do when a twig snaps and something big walks into the clearing.

I got to my feet, sure that everybody was staring at me. I took a peek as I collected my stuff.

Four guys, two in those shiny Rolling Stones jackets with the big tongues on the back, and two in sleeveless muscle T's, eyed me. They were the kind who spent a lot of time in front of the mirror working on their laser gaze. The quad was completely quiet now. Everybody was watching.

I took a deep breath, one that shuddered on its way in. *Oh, man.*

"What do you think you're doin'?" He left big spaces between the words, just like he'd been taught at Intimidation School.

It was hard keeping my voice steady, so I just looked at his sloping, hairless chest. "Going to my homeroom. I tripped."

"By cutting across the Senior Patio?"

I looked down at the bricks. "I didn't know," I stammered.

He looked pained. He tested his tall blond hair to make sure it was at attention. "That's no excuse."

Oh, great: the first day of school and a fat lip. Mom would come unglued. "I'll go around, okay?"

"Too late now, Fag Face."

"C'mon. I'm new here."

"What's your name, new boy?"

"Tony."

"Tony Baloney? Tony Phony?"

"Candelaria."

"Candelabra?"

That cracked them up. One of the muscle shirts said, "What do you do, man, hang around the ballroom all day?"

I watched them guffaw and snort and slap at one another's hands. I just waited, my eyes on their big, heavy shoes.

"I want you to do something," snapped the leader of the pack.

"Like what?"

I could feel the tension drain out of the air as most of the kids went back to whispering or eating or lying about the summer. They were still watching, but there probably wasn't going to be a fight after all.

"See that babe over there with the sign, the one standing

by the fag artist and the Toulouse-Lautrec of the wheelchair set? Her name is Jordan."

I looked at the girl who'd yelled at me, the girl in the black dress, the dress with the padlocks. "So?"

"So go over there and tell her I'm available tonight." He handed me a stick of Juicy Fruit gum. "If she's like undecided, give her this piece of gum."

"No beads, no mirrors, no wampum?"

He shoved one balled fist right under my nose.

"Okay, okay."

Jordan, who'd been watching all this, grinned down at her ponytailed friend in the red, high-tech wheelchair, then up at the other guy, whose scraggly beard was black, but everything else was blue: Dodger cap, bandanna, shirt, pants, shoes.

"If only," she said as I got close, "I'd been recording the sound of bodies hitting bricks for an acoustic art piece. You went down pretty hard."

"That guy wants you to—"

"I know what Barry wants."

I noticed how thrashed her Dr. Martens were and how the heavy locks tugged at her dress.

"So will you do it?" I asked.

"Barry's only going to hit you once," she teased.

"C'mon. It's my first day. Please."

"So let's say I help you out here. What do I get? Will you buy one of my kits?"

"I'm plenty chaste already. I don't need a kit."

"Well, then . . ."

"Oh, give him a break," urged the Dodger cap.

The kid in the wheelchair grinned up at me. "She's harmless. Really."

She took a deep breath. "All right, all right. Just tell Barry that if I were to accept this gift, it could begin a chain of events that would destroy my life."

Her two friends started to grin.

"Okay," I said dubiously.

"Because that stick of gum has sugar in it, right? And sugar causes cavities. So I chew this gum and get a cavity in one of my front teeth. I go to a cut-rate dentist because that's all I can afford. When I'm under anesthesia he caresses my breast and I wake up with a gnawing, inexplicable sense of shame and a long gold fang because women with long gold fangs are his thing. Shunned by my friends and banned from school by a vice-principal who fears classroom disruption by fanged girls, I live with a pack of wolves where fangs make sense. I'm claimed not by the alpha wolf, but by the omega wolf, who just lies around the den all night playing show tunes. So there I am—filthy, frustrated, and howling at the moon all because I took that one stick of gum."

As she exchanged high fives with her pals, I said, "I'll tell him you said no."

"Make it easy on yourself. I don't think that nose of yours can take one more punch."

I trekked back to the Smirking Quartet. "It took a while, but she said—"

"I know. I know. That's what she always says." Barry waved me away as the first bell rang. "And stay off the Senior Patio!"

"Hey, there!" someone yelled.

I watched a woman come down the stairs. She wore black slacks and a black blouse under a white cardigan. Her graying hair looked like number nine from the Hair Affair menu. She held out one hand.

"Ms. Christophe, assistant principal."

"Tony Candelaria, new kid."

"Oh, yes. I've seen your records." She gestured toward my tormentors. "I was watching, and I just thought I'd let you take care of things your own way. If I stepped in, they might never let it drop. This way, it's finished." She looked me over. "Seems like you handled yourself pretty well."

"I can grovel with the best of them."

One hand landed on my shoulder: the Consoling Grip straight out of the *Assistant Principal's Handbook*. Then she nodded to her left. "By the way, that's Mr. Emery, your principal."

I followed her gaze. Mr. Emery was lecturing a student. The grown-up's suit was black and looked hard. The kid's face was white as cottage cheese. Black and white: the school colors.

"He's strict, but fair."

"Okay."

"But you might want to see me first if you have a problem."

I nodded.

Her eyes narrowed like Superman's when he was about to kick in his X-ray vision. "I know it's disorienting to be the new kid," she said.

"I'm used to it."

"Compounded by what happened to your father."

I corrected her. "Stepfather."

"Stepfather." Her hand tightened on my shoulder. "We're all sorry."

All? She and Mr. Christophe? Everybody in the school? The world?

I bit my tongue. "Thanks."

Then she rummaged in one pants pocket, tried her cardigan, and finally came up with a hall pass although—technically—there weren't any halls, only sidewalks.

20

Just then a bunch of kids went by. One of them laughed and said, "What bullshit."

Ms. Christophe snapped, "Randy!" She pulled out a pad of yellow slips, circled something, passed it to Randy. "Detention."

"What for?" He stared at the piece of paper. "I didn't say anything vulgar. Everybody says bullshit."

"Another of those disclaimers, and you're looking at Saturday school."

Randy sighed and turned away. Ms. Christophe smiled at me.

"Where were we?" she asked.

"You gave me this pass."

"Right, right. So I'll drop by your homeroom and say you're talking to the counselor. Afterward, you can just go to first period."

"I don't need to talk to a counselor."

"Everyone needs an ed plan. But if you'd like to talk about something else, Mr. Passmore is available for that, too."

I must have looked blank.

"Emotional things. Feelings. Problems. Self-esteem. Mr. Passmore's door is always open."

"Must be drafty," I mumbled.

"Humor is a great healer."

After an upbeat handshake, I went for guidance. Inside every room I passed, the kids were milling around. The teachers sat at their desks looking stunned: it was the first day of school for them, too.

Mr. Passmore's door *was* open, so I got a quick glance before I knocked. He'd made a little home for himself in there: Mr. Coffee, Ms. Microwave, a big high-backed chair, Bolivian wall hangings, a spider plant, a mug with Barney the dinosaur on it.

He was cherubic in a big way, with a headful of curls, bowl-full-of-jelly-type stomach, short pudgy fingers. A loose white shirt covered his chest, and I could see green Birkenstocks sticking out from under his cluttered desk. Any empty wall space was filled with travel posters. Had he been to those mountains and beaches, or did he just want to go?

I tapped on the door frame with one knuckle.

"Tony?"

"Yeah, how'd you know?"

He touched his forehead with all ten fingertips. "The Great Passmore knows all, sees all." Then he grinned impishly. "Also, there are only three new students and I've seen two of them." He pointed to the empty chair. Beside it stood a low table with two open boxes of Kleenex. Do kids cry when they can't get in to Stanford?

"Students tell me things," he said like I'd asked out loud. "Personal stuff sometimes." Then he plucked a file from somewhere and let it fall open.

"You move a lot."

"Yes."

"But your grades are good."

"They're okay."

"Have you thought about your future—college, things like that?"

"A little, I guess."

"We have a good state college nearby."

"We're not staying around here."

He sat back, pushing his glasses up on his nose. "You're moving again? How do you feel about that?"

I shrugged. His carpet had an odd pattern that reminded me of knives and guns, but I sure wasn't going to tell him that.

"Tony? How do you—"

"What's the point of feeling anything about it, Mr. Passmore. It is what it is, right?"

He leaned forward and made a little Eiffel Tower with his fingers. "Well, Tony, I don't know about that."

Just then the bell rang. I was on my feet like Sly Stallone as Rocky Balboa.

"Let's talk about an ed plan, anyway," he said, standing up, too. "You might end up staying. You never know."

"Believe me. I know."

When I got to E200, I tugged my T-shirt straight, made sure my fly was zipped, then peeked in. The room was mostly full already. I could see the usual maps of Chaucer's England featuring dressed-up knights riding dressed-up horses. There were big framed pictures of Cesar Chávez, Martin Luther King, Jr., the Kennedys, and some astronauts—all as dead as the Middle Ages.

"Hey!"

Everybody looked at me like I was the one who'd yelled.

"Over here." Jordan motioned, both arms waving like she was helping to park a 747. The locks on her dress gleamed in the sharp morning light.

I glanced around. There was one empty seat in the room—right next to her. Everybody watched me walk. They watched me sit down and put my book bag between her chair and mine. I scooted closer to the window and looked out.

She tapped me on the arm and pointed to the kid in the high-tech wheelchair. "We're all artists. This is Hector." She half turned around. "And this is Blue."

I could see out of the corner of my eye that Hector just nodded, but Blue started in: "Before you ask, I've got six brothers and sisters. To make things easier—laundry, in particular—everybody got a color. If it's blue, it's mine; pink is Diane's; green is Thad's, etcetera."

"Blue's art hangs on the wall; Hector's into graphics." She kicked my chair. "Hey! What's out there? What are you, a bird-watcher?"

" 'His art hangs on the wall,' " I repeated to show I'd been paying attention.

"Right. Good. Now, are you an artist?"

"No."

"How about sports?"

"Not really."

"Girls."

"Not exactly."

"You gay?"

"No!"

"Do you like movies?"

"I don't get to go much."

"Do you read books?"

"Not yet, but I can follow along and point at the horsie."

"Who are you mad at?"

"I'm not mad at anybody."

She cocked her head and pointed to one ear. "Tone says it all. And sound is my medium right now, so don't try and fool me."

"Great, two shrinks in a row." I reached for my book bag.

She held me down with one hand. "Relax. We'll talk about something noninflammatory: how do you like West Paradise?"

I pulled a book from my bag. "I need to read the introduction."

"Hey, I saved your life out there in the quad. Talk to me."

"You saved my life? You said that guy was just going to hit me once."

She smashed one fist into the other open palm. "One *big* hit."

"She's harmless," Hector advised.

"You keep saying that."

Jordan shook her head so hard her close-cropped hair moved. "I'm not either harmless. I'm like Vampira." She arched her fingers, showed me her front teeth, and mangled a Transylvanian accent. "I need fresh blood."

"She's stuck on a piece," Blue explained.

"I'm not stuck!" she insisted.

"She's stuck."

"It helps me to talk to new people, that's all. They've got new points of view. They've got leftover geographic electromagnetic impulses. I can use leftover geographic electromagnetic impulses."

"Indulge her," Blue advised.

Jordan locked onto me again. "So how do you like West Paradise?"

"There's too many trees, okay? And it's too clean. It's like totalitarian clean."

"Nice. 'Totalitarian clean' is nice." She motioned like I owed her a dollar. "C'mon. I want more."

"Hey, this isn't a McDonald's. You said talk and I talked." I turned to Hector and Blue. "You guys heard me, right?"

"More," said Jordan.

"What about?"

"Anything. It's not content I'm interested in, okay?"

She acted edgy and kind of wired. I wondered if she was on something. It seemed easiest to play along.

"Well, I thought L.A. would be—"

"Well, we're not L.A. This is a suburb. A superb suburb."

"Anyway," Hector said without looking up from the sketchbook in his lap, "there's Compton, Brentwood, Playa del Rey, San Dimas, and etcetera. But there really isn't an L.A. except the one in your head."

"Well, the one in my head had more graffiti and gangs and stuff. My mom keeps telling me how I can get shot for blinking."

"I know where you can get shot," said Hector, "but we'll have to drive fifteen miles."

Blue shook his head. "No reason to drive to South Central. There's guys in Paradise who'll shoot you *and* jack your car."

I remembered seeing a football schedule. "Are those the same guys West Paradise plays?"

"It's brutal," said Blue. "Pro scouts show up at all their games; they drafted one kid right in the middle of shop class. He just dropped the knife he was making and walked out."

"We've got Bobby Xi," Hector murmured.

I followed Blue's eyes to a bulked-up Chinese kid with a ponytail.

"Bobby's too sweet," said Jordan. "They're going to walk all over him." She scooted her desk closer. "Talk some more."

I shook my head. I was just about to see if I could request a new homeroom when Rochelle from the chastity club marched up. She straightened her coveralls indignantly. "We don't think your dress is very funny, Jordan."

"Wasn't meant to be funny," she replied.

"I can't wait till Ms. Christophe makes you take that stupid chain off."

Jordan shot to her feet. "Let her try. I get to wear this just like you get to indoctrinate the masses, okay?"

"My sister got pregnant this summer, Jordan. So what I'm doing is a lot more important than some stupid painting."

Jordan charged right up to Rochelle. "What? More important than art? Are you crazy? You're a good painter. Let Planned Parenthood march around and hand stuff out. You should be working on—"

"You don't understand, Jordan."

"Hey, you're the one who doesn't understand."

Rochelle frowned and stamped her foot. "Jordan, I hate you sometimes."

"Hey, hey, hey," Jordan said. "If anybody should hate anybody, we should hate you. You blew us off. You're the one who's not going to live at the Ironworks anymore. You're not going to be part of a quartet of rising young artists destined to make their mark early and to continue . . ."

Hector made the *T* sign for time out. "This is just the first day of school. Let's save some conflict for midterms."

But Jordan wasn't having any of that. ". . . to present a broad range of compelling and accessible ideas."

Rochelle backed up a step, but not because she was scared. "You're not exactly the one to be talking about compelling and accessible anything. All you do is tell everybody who'll listen about what a great artist you are. But who wins the prizes?" She pointed. "Blue, that's who."

"Hey," Blue said, "one prize doesn't mean—"

"And who's got his drawings at DC Comics, not you."

"DC is *looking* at them," said Hector. "It's not like—"

Rochelle cut him off, too. "Where are your paintings, Jordan? Where are your drawings? Do you ever make anything that anybody can see? Or do you just talk about what you're going to do and how wonderful you're going to be at it?"

Jordan was as red-faced as Rochelle. Blue looked out the window. Hector buried his thin face in his book. What a crew. If I didn't want to feel bad about leaving West Paradise, this was the bunch to hang with, all right.

Just then our teacher tapped on her desk with a Bic pen. She was narrow as a green bean and wore a black dress, like she'd just come from a vegetarian funeral.

27

"Ladies, ladies," she said. "Settle down. Everybody take your seats, please."

She strolled to the board and wrote MRS. ABBEY on it. There was a bust of Shakespeare beside her roll book. When she put one hand on Will's pate and slid him back from the edge of the desk, it was like a huge gearshift, and she was putting the new semester into drive.

〰〰〰

The rest of the day was the usual blur: lists of recommended and required reading, homework, essays due Monday, term papers in six weeks. Most of the teachers seemed okay: one really nice, one really tough, the others in between.

At three-thirty I skirted the precious Senior Patio and angled past the Snack Shack. Across the street were the gym, baseball field, tennis courts, and a beauty of a pool with those colorful floating lane dividers that look like DNA.

Still in their Stones jackets and muscle shirts, Barry and his henchmen were shooting baskets. I had to go past them, so I shifted the book bag onto my left shoulder like a duffel and tried to—as it were—sneak through customs.

"Hey, Candelabra! Take a shot."

The basketball sailed my way, landed with a thunk, bounced and hit me in the butt. That cracked them up completely.

I stopped, scooped up the ball, and walked onto the court. Those guys had been watching too many MTV videos; they stood around, hips cocked, attitude installed, ready to snarl something that would go platinum before Christmas.

I got just inside three-point range, dribbled a few times to get the feel of the ball, then tried a one-handed set shot. Swish! I breathed a sigh of relief.

"Holy Patrick Ewing!" shouted Barry. "Come back here, Candlepower. Do that again."

I was already walking away. "I gotta get home."

"Nah, c'mon. We'll go two on three. You and me against them."

I cut across the street at just the right speed—not scared, not arrogant—and scooped up my bag. "Another time. I've really got to get home."

As I turned the corner, I knew I'd been lucky—well, a little lucky. When Mom and Bill and I lived in Daly City, I'd played an awful lot of driveway basketball. The house we'd leased had a backboard over the garage. Bill had played college ball for Rice. He was a hundred times better than me, but a good teacher.

When we were too tired for one-on-one, we'd play horse, and sometimes he'd just stand under the basket and feed me the ball. I'd sink one after another, backing up a little after every five-in-a-row.

I missed playing ball. I missed playing ball with him.

I stopped outside our condo. It was a flat-faced stucco. They were all as identical as sheets.

Just then a door opened and our neighbor Mr. Reed and his son Johnny came out, both of them with tennis rackets.

I watched them walk all the way to their car, then looked for my house key. Inside, I dropped my book bag with a thump. "Mom!"

"Here, honey."

She was lying on the couch, covered by a cactus-colored throw. "I was dreaming," she said. "I was somewhere strange and all your fathers were there."

"The Houston Astrodome, maybe."

She pretended to be unamused as she stood up and kissed me on the cheek. "How was school?"

"Not exactly the Palace of the Mountain Gods, but okay, I guess."

"I liked school," she said dreamily. "I was popular."

"You're still popular, or you would be if you'd get out."

" 'Get out,' " she repeated. "Isn't that what dogs do?"

"You know what I mean. You said yesterday you felt a lot better."

Mom reached up and made that tsssking sound. "I still don't understand why you got all your beautiful hair cut off."

"An impulse. I'm just an impulsive guy."

"Did you eat lunch?"

"I took chicken salad, remember? But I saw what passes for food: it was grim. And if that isn't bad enough, there's dancing from twelve-thirty to one."

"Where's dancing?"

"At the school. In the cafeteria. There's a jukebox, and if you want to you can get up and make a fool out of yourself."

"Did you dance?"

"Are you kidding?" I stood up. "If anybody should dance, it's you. You never get any exercise."

"Are you rusty—is that it?"

I walked around the coffee table. "What am I, the Tin Man? No, I'm not rusty."

"Dancing is a good way to meet people, that's all."

"I don't want to meet people. I just want to get these four months over with."

"Well, did you at least talk to anybody?"

I thought of the jerks who'd tried to terrorize me. I thought of my guidance counselor. I thought of Jordan, Blue, Hector, Rochelle.

"No."

"You didn't talk to any of the other students?"

"No."

"But you had to sit by somebody."

"There's a pole for new kids. I sat on top of that."

"Tony, please. I've been by myself all day."

I put up both hands in the classic I Surrender pose. "All right, all right. I met a bunch of artists: one in a wheelchair, one named after a primary color, a former artist who is now professionally celibate, and one who'd wrapped certain parts of herself in a chain."

She arched her brows. "They're not gang members, are they?"

"Believe me, gang members is the last thing they are."

"They sound interesting."

"What they are is weird."

She patted the couch. "Well, it was just the first day."

I looked toward the laundry room. "And what'd you do today? Not fold clothes?"

She looked at the big pile. "I meant to. I just forgot, I guess. Sometimes I don't know where the time goes." She sighed heavily. "I'm glad you're home. I missed you." She reached for my hand.

I pulled away. "Why don't you get cleaned up before we eat."

"I'm not going to eat tonight. I feel fat." She watched me go into the kitchen. "You're supposed to say, 'You don't look fat.'"

"Consider it said. You've still got to eat."

"Is it *camerónes el diablo*?" she asked.

I nodded. "If you want."

"Well, maybe I'll soak in the tub for a little while."

"Sure."

I watched her trudge upstairs, then checked the refrigerator. Just below the shrimp was a beautiful eggplant and some crook-necked squash as yellow as the borders of a *National Geographic*.

There was some cold chicken left, too, so before I got down to work I made half a sandwich with sourdough bread and Dijon mustard and put it on one of the new dishes from Macy's.

Every plate had a rooster on it, a big noisy-looking guy. I'd been glad when Mom picked them out. They seemed lively, and I hoped that was a good sign.

I fell into the nearest chair and picked up the remote: a weatherman on KMEX pointed to Kansas and the word *Tormentas*, somebody waved a magic mop, parents on a talk show yelled at other parents about child rearing while their own daughters slumped and chewed their split ends.

I started to think about the fluttery winglike pages of a cookbook, the deep gong of one heavy pan against another.

But first I needed to fold the laundry. I didn't like to cook when things were messy. So I separated Mom's stuff from mine.

That left some dirty jeans and towels to wash; to save time I took off the shirt I had on and added it to the pile. I was checking its pockets when I came across a wadded-up paper: the number for Confess-O-Rama.

I threw it on the counter, measured a cup of soap, got the machine started. Then I surfed across the same fifty-two channels, took the green peppers and onions out of the refrigerator, and looked at the phone number again.

Why not? Mom couldn't hear. She was resting. And I was cooking.

"Welcome to Confess-O-Rama," said a husky, muffled voice. "We're here twenty-four hours a day, seven days a week. Your anonymity is guaranteed. Nothing is too gross, melancholy, or delusional. So c'mon. What's festering down there? What do you need to get off your mind before your heart just blows up in your chest?"

I listened through the beep. Then I asked, "Anybody there? I mean a real person?" I could hear the tape machine. "Not that I want to talk to a real person. I was just kind of checking. Just, I don't know—checking. I don't know why. It's not like anything earthshaking has happened to me in the five whole days I've been here, unless you count getting hassled on the first day of school."

I liked it that nobody said anything back. I liked the little hiss the tape made as it remembered what I said—unconditional indifference.

"Well, okay. I'll confess this much: I don't want to join any clubs, I don't want to make any friends, and I for sure don't want a girlfriend. But do the kids I meet have to be so weird? Do I have to sit by the most irritating girl in the world, and does she have to smell like turpentine?"

Monday morning, Mom's bedroom door was closed, but there was a note downstairs.

The early bird gets the worm! I've gone to look for a job!
I'll eat breakfast, I promise!

It was nice in the kitchen by myself. Sun angled through the window, warmed the blue tile, and bounced off the chrome faucets. I washed some spinach, whipped a couple of eggs, and got out my omelet pan. I liked to fold the eggs over onto the green leaves, tuck them in, and make a gift for myself.

Then I sat at the counter and looked at *Hamlet*, the play where his father's ghost shows up on the ramparts of the castle. If Shakespeare had written *Tony*, there'd have to be a quartet of ghosts in the mall at Elsinore.

A little later, I took the same route to school. There were the same antiques, seventy-two hours older; the same baggy-pantsed kids strutting like the ones on MTV; the same bike riders and skateboarders; the same posters on the same ancient trees.

Not far from school, a middle-aged guy in a blue Toyota pickup was tossing papers onto every lawn, and I wondered what the news was like in West Paradise: probably front-page stuff like somebody was taking a nap when an orange fell into his hammock.

"Tony!"

Hector was sitting in his wheelchair by a wall of junk food machines. They all had little mirrors right above the selections so you could check the tooth decay or count the new zits while you pulled the knob for still another creamy, dreamy, marshmallow, caramel, nut log.

I thought about just waving, then heading for the bathroom or something. But, if you want to know the whole truth and nothing but the truth, I probably liked hearing somebody call my name, you know? Somebody besides my mom.

He motioned for my book bag, piled it on his lap, and pointed to a battered spot down by the first *s* in *snacks*. "Kick this thing for me, will you? It took my money."

I gave it a whack, and we heard a quarter clatter into the coin return.

"Cool," he said, fishing it out, trying again and—this time—getting a candy bar. "Want a bite?"

"No, thanks."

"So you're like Jordan's dad—Mr. No Junk Food."

"I don't know about that." Students milled around, rubbing against one another, banging antlers, grazing. Before I retrieved my book bag, I tucked in my T-shirt.

"Did you get a deal on white ones?" Hector asked.

Just then Rochelle—wearing her Worth Waiting For T-shirt over a red turtleneck—bounced our way. She had long curls, the kind girls wear on PBS when they're riding in a carriage.

"Tony, how are you?" she asked.

"Okay, I guess."

"The meeting's today at three-thirty."

"I don't think so, Rochelle."

"I'd come," said Hector, "but—"

Rochelle finished for him. "Jordan."

"Yeah."

She looked at the ground. "Did I let you guys down?"

Hector shrugged. "It's okay. That Ironworks thing is a nice plan, but I don't know how realistic it is: four kooky kids and their madcap adventures in the world of alternative art. Life isn't a sitcom."

"I think what I'm doing with the club is important."

He reached for her hand. "It is."

"Painting's hard," Rochelle said. "Sometimes I think I did it just because Jordan wanted me to."

"You're a pretty good artist."

She shook her head. "Not like you."

"Well, I don't have much else to do."

"The chair doesn't matter. You were drawing in grade school."

"So were you."

"Unicorns."

"Not after Jordan got hold of you."

They both laughed. Then Rochelle said, "She makes me so mad sometimes." But she didn't sound mad. Then she leaned and gave Hector a hug, smiled at me, and split.

As she trudged away, Hector rolled closer. "Could I draw something," he said half to himself, "about peers pressuring their peers to resist peer pressure?"

I shrugged.

"And," he went on, "if I did, would it do as much good as actually telling somebody not to fool around?" He looked up. "But you're not into art, are you."

"Not much."

"What are you into?"

"Mobility. I'm into being mobile."

Hector nodded. "Cool answer. Want to be friends?"

That made me laugh. "Is that how it's done?"

"Why not? You're straight; you're fairly witty; and you're obviously on the run from the fashion police, which gives you that attractive outlaw image. So speaking for a trio of rising young artists, I thought I'd put in my bid first."

"Is there a big demand for friends around here?"

Hector looked at the spotless campus, the spotless kids, their spotless smiles. "Entropy will get you if you don't watch out. It's real comfortable here: clean, safe, pretty affluent. Almost everybody goes away to college, then comes home at holidays and eats the big meal. If you're not careful, you're brain-dead." He pointed. "Anyway, sit down. We'll have an orgy of self-revelation: I'll tell you a secret, you tell me one."

"I don't have any secrets."

"Yeah, right." Hector's hair was black like mine but even thicker and about ten times as long. He pulled his ponytail around and tucked the end into his shirt pocket. "I'll start."

I glanced around. "Look, Hector . . ."

"Oh, relax. You know how lifeguards at the pool are always yelling, 'No running'?"

"Yeah."

"I was running. Next thing you know, I'm falling; next thing I'm the only guy sitting down for the national anthem."

"Jeez."

"My sentiments exactly. And guess who saved my life, I mean not counting the doctors and rehab and all that."

I shook my head.

"Jordan. My parents are at Holy Family praying, right? And don't get me wrong: my folks are cool and the prayers probably helped. But Jordan immediately wants to do some art piece, some performance thing called *Legs*."

"Ouch."

Hector just grinned. "She starts taking all kinds of Polaroids, has me talking into a tape recorder, eventually gets me over to her place. You haven't met her dad yet, right?"

"Right, I just—"

"Very cool guy. Talented out the yin-yang. Works his butt off. But weird. I'm two days out of rehab and he looks down at me and says, 'How does this loss serve you? Where does it point your work?'"

"Are you kidding? What'd you do?"

"I listened. Before the accident I was kind of on the water polo team, kind of into journalism, kind of an artist. After I talked to Drew Archer, I got focused." He took the last bite of his candy bar. "They're good questions, aren't they? How does this loss serve you? Where does it point your work?"

Man, I had loss to spare. And my work. What was that?

Just then I heard whistles and whoops. Hector pushed off, heading for the wide gap that opened onto the street.

"C'mon. Let's get a free burrito."

I showed him my book bag. "No, I should really—"

"Oh, come on, or I'll roll over your foot."

So I followed Hector, who shouted, "Handicapped parking. Make way." When we got almost to the street, he waved me past.

I looked over the hair and the baseball caps. "No, you go. Jordan's up there."

"So? Burrow on in and make room for me."

I slipped in behind her and Blue. When she squished up against me as Hector rolled by, I could smell a weird combination of paint thinner, Arrid Extra Dry, and flat-out tiredness.

"You don't have a Coke on you, do you?" she asked, half-turning around. "I've been up all night."

I just stared at the street.

"Tony. Come in, Tony. Mission control requests a Coke."

I just shook my head as a black pickup with chrome mag wheels pulled up almost headlight to headlight with a dusty old Dodge Aries.

On the side of the pickup, over a shine so deep it was like outer space, were the words COFFIN CORRAL. The Dodge had KGAB scrawled on its door. When the driver gunned his engine, it sounded like a Hamilton Beach blender.

"That's Sheila Larson in the pickup," Blue said. "Barry's mom."

I watched her reach back into the truck and give her son a handful of something. He jogged toward the crowd, wearing an old Queen T-shirt over his big fat gut.

"What's going on, anyway?" I whispered to Blue.

"Every now and then," said Jordan, "she drives around

town in that thing and hands out burrito coupons courtesy of the Coffin Corral."

"I was talking to Blue."

Jordan was ragged, sooty-eyed, and jittery. "Oh," she said, "excuse me. I am so sorry. Please forgive me."

"Incidentally," said Hector, "Sheila was married to Larry, the guy in the beater."

"Who's Larry?"

"Well, Larry Deluxe is KGAB's number one talk show guy."

"KGAB's only talk show guy," corrected Hector.

"Larry's okay," said Blue. "At least he's on our side."

"Well, Sheila's the coffin queen. You go in this warehouse," Hector explained, "pick out your favorite pine box, then haggle with the saleswomen."

"All women," said Jordan, "top to bottom. The whole organization."

I stared at Barry's mom, who, in her black hat and black blouse, was dressed like death's foreman.

"People drive in from the Valley just to roam around in her warehouse. It's weird, but very—as they say—L.A."

Larry stepped out of his car and glared. "This," said Blue, "is what passes for *Clash of the Titans* here in West Paradise."

As Larry stalked past, I checked out the stuff on his dashboard: newspapers, manila folders. McDonald's cups, a KGAB baseball hat. Larry himself could have been sixth runner-up in the Robert Redford look-alike contest. He had a ton of blond hair, that same rugged complexion, and actually a fairly dazzling smile.

He nodded to his former wife, who leaned against the shiny fender, arms crossed while her son worked the crowd. "I'll be out of here in a sec," she said.

Larry adjusted his rose-colored sunglasses. "Take your

time." He yawned real big to show time meant nothing to him.

Ms. Larson turned, waved to everyone, then patched out in reverse no less, leaving long strips of Michelin's best on the concrete as the crowd cheered.

"Everybody," Larry said, waving for silence. "Everybody over here, okay? Kids?" He looked our way. "Fellas?" Then he tilted his glasses and peered over them. "Blue, is that you? Come over here and bring your friends, okay?"

Blue nudged me, kicked Hector's wheelchair lightly, and we shuffled forward.

Larry beamed at Jordan. "How are you?" he asked. "How's your dad?"

Jordan shrugged. "Okay, I guess."

"You're still mad, aren't you?"

"No."

"I would've voted for you."

"Thanks a lot, Larry," she said.

Larry looked down at his scuffed shoes, that soft-looking kind called, I think, Hush Puppies. "Well, you're the one who was . . ."

Just then Barry strolled over. He looped one thick arm around his father's neck. "You want me to get 'em for you, Dad?"

"They're fine. They're coming."

"HEY! Get over here, everybody. I mean it." He pointed left, then right, and his henchmen swung around the crowd like sinister sheepdogs.

As most of the kids oozed back toward us, I whispered to Blue, "What didn't Jordan win?"

"KGAB had a student art thing," she said.

I couldn't believe she'd heard me. "Man, no wonder you want to work with sound! You've got ears like a fox."

Jordan grinned. "And Larry was one of the judges. I did a life-size Barbie on her deathbed called *The Voluptuousness of Fiasco*. Blue did a painting, a really nice one." She shrugged. "He won."

Blue poked her hard with a sharp elbow. "Tell him the whole thing."

Jordan looked at her paint-splattered hands. "I didn't exactly get there on time."

"She came in," Blue said, "with this incredible piece of hers on a gurney right *after* the awards ceremony."

"And then," Hector added, "she went in the hospital."

"For a couple of days," Jordan said. "Big deal. I just slept a lot."

"Everybody shut up now!" Barry looked around menacingly. "Okay, Dad."

Larry held up both hands like he was silencing the multitudes. "I'm going to do a week," he announced, "of high school talk radio pretty soon, okay? And I want you guys to help me out. What do you want to chat about? I'm not eighteen, I'm not in the demo, you guys are in the demo. So call the station or just come on up here and tell me today. As of now I'm doing . . ." He began to pat his pockets. "Wait a second."

Larry turned, dove into the front seat of his Dodge, and started to dig. Papers rose behind him; a book flew into the backseat; folders flapped their pale wings.

I looked longingly at the Art Building, but I was trapped.

"Here we go. Here we go." And Larry began to pass out fliers.

Jordan sniffed hers. "Done on a mimeograph," she said. "Nothing like cutting edge technology."

"So let's see here," Larry said. "Tell me what you think about these topics, okay? Let's start with school uniforms."

The crowd muttered.

"That's a no. Okay, how about birth control on campus?"

"How about chastity?" bellowed Rochelle.

Larry wrote that down. "Bilingual education?" he asked.

"*Sí,*" shouted some smart aleck, and everybody laughed.

"Censorship?"

"No!"

"Great," said Larry. "Thanks. And how about one more. There's this kid in Beverly Hills with some kind of multiple personality thing who's claiming that since only one of his personalities failed the math final the rest of them should graduate. What do you think?"

He had them going now. They roared, "Graduate!"

Just then the first bell rang, and Barry dismissed us, just like it was his idea. "Go cellular, you guys. Call between classes. I mean it. Starting tomorrow I don't want to see anybody at the break who hasn't got a phone in his hand."

Then all of us turned and headed for class. Halfway there Barry jogged up and started to hand out the last of the coupons.

"Two for you, Jordan, cause size forty coveralls splattered with paint and gunk get me hot."

"Bite me," she said amiably, tucking them in one huge pocket.

He held a yellow coupon out toward me, then pulled it back, then held it out again. "Did I see you on the Senior Patio again, Candlepuck? Cause if I did, no free burrito."

"Bite him, too," said Jordan.

Barry gave me the finger, of course, as he threw the rest of his coupons into the air. He nudged one of his buddies as a girl in a crop top leaned over.

Jordan stopped, scribbled something on a scrap of paper, drew a quick sketch, frowned at it, then followed Hector back to class.

We spent the morning learning the kind of things that turn up on "High School Jeopardy," so at noon it was a relief to throw my book bag in a locker and head for the cafeteria. The smell that had almost turned me away on Friday hit me again—grease, cheap meat, and vegetables boiled until they all looked like cauliflower. I knew that food. It was made deep in the bowels of the earth by trolls, then piped into every high school in the United States.

And the noise! The slam-dance of silverware and trays. Football players, each with ten desserts ringing the cowering entrée. Girls shrieking like the high priest was about to pick out a virgin for the volcano god.

I got myself a carton of milk and settled into a little table off by itself. In a dim corner. All I needed was a dunce cap.

Somehow Jordan found me.

"Can I sit down?" she asked. "What are you doin' over here all by yourself? What are you eating?"

"One, no. Two, I'm fine by myself. Three, leftover shrimp."

She laughed. "That was semiclever. I've got a good feeling about you and my work." Before I could stop her she reached past me and peeked under the lid of my Tupperware bowl. "Where'd you get this? Or for that matter, what *is* this?"

"Camerónes el diablo."

"Where'd you get *that*?"

"I made it."

"You cooked it? How did you do that?"

"It's easy." I pointed to her cafeteria-created sandwich, still wrapped in plastic. "That thing could've been suffocated by a serial killer. So don't start with me about food, okay? Because you don't know anything about it."

Jordan stood up straight. "All right! Signs of life."

Just then Ms. Christophe came striding up and put one hand on my shoulder. "Tony, how are you getting along?"

"Okay."

"Making friends?"

"Tony just proposed," Jordan said, "but I told him my first love was Art."

Ms. Christophe smiled indulgently. "I missed you this summer, Jordan. Everything was so quiet."

When an old Natalie Merchant cut came pounding out of a jukebox, Jordan yelled, "Where'd you used to live?"

"Which time?"

"Last time, I guess."

"Daly City. Just outside of San Francisco."

"Show me how they dance up there."

"Are you kidding?"

"No. Show me."

"They dance the same. Everybody dances the same."

"No, they don't. Artists need breadth, so I want to see regional differences. I might want to do a piece called . . ." She snapped her fingers for inspiration. "*The Discrepancy Boogie.* Or something like that." She gripped my wrist and pulled. "So c'mon."

I pulled back.

"I'll tell you what. Show me how they dance and I'll never bother you again."

"You will, too."

"Maybe, but you can't be sure. I at least *might* never bother you again. For sure not about dancing."

I stared at her. God, she should have put herself in an art piece—some kind of perpetual motion grinding machine. She just wore me down.

Jordan hopped up and down. "C'mon, Tony!"

44

"One dance. Just one."

"Fine."

I followed her toward the edge of the crowded floor because some kids, led by Barry, of course, were starting to bounce off of one another like the cafeteria was the mosh pit of the trendiest club in town.

Then I looked around and shook my head. "I changed my mind. This isn't a good idea."

"You," said Jordan, "are like a little forest creature. I feel like I ought to have a handful of watercress to lure you out of the shadows. Just show me."

"Okay, okay."

I held out my arms. She stepped into me, her left hand on my shoulder, her right palm flat against mine. I counted out loud, "One, two, three, four," as we negotiated the standard box.

She dropped my hands like they were hot. "Oh, come on. I learned this in third grade."

Just then somebody screamed. I heard a cafeteria tray hit the floor. A wave of students swept toward us. Jordan slipped, grabbed hard, and tore my shirt pocket as my feet were knocked right out from under me.

〰〰〰

Waking up was the most delicious feeling: warm, woozy, heavy—like somebody had been telling me a story and I'd drifted off.

Then I opened my eyes. A nurse, white as an iceberg, held something under my nose, and a circle of faces stared down at me.

"He's all right," said the iceberg.

Jordan knelt beside me. "Either you got the wind knocked

45

out of you," she said. "Or you were showing me the Daly City Death Spiral."

I sat up and felt my stomach. "I'm okay."

I heard Ms. Christophe shoo the crowd away as Barry squatted down beside me. "What a weenie," he hissed.

Blue held out one hand. I grabbed it and found myself standing up.

"I'll take him for a little walk in the fresh air," said Jordan.

"That might be best." Ms. Christophe looked at the big, pleasant nurse, who nodded and mumbled something about my personal physician.

Jordan tugged at me. "C'mon."

"But," I began, "I feel . . ."

"Terrible. I know. Just lean on me."

Outside looked like something a little kid might paint: one white cloud sat in a perfectly blue sky.

"You okay?" Jordan asked, steering me toward the parking lot.

"Uh-huh. Little woozy. Man, I hate that kind of dancing—that slam dancing, mosh pit, stage diving crap."

"Well, you're a survivor. Next it'll be Nine Inch Nails concerts."

"In your dreams." Then I rubbed my face real hard with both hands. "I'm really okay. We should turn around."

She took a deep breath. "Are you kidding? We're out of school while everybody else is lined up like freight cars memorizing the haircut of the kids in front of them."

"Freight cars wouldn't memorize anything. That's a mixed metaphor."

"Oh, excuse me."

The world was coming back to normal. I felt my T-shirt across my shoulders, my cinched belt, my shoes.

46

Jordan pointed at an old green Honda wagon. "Say hello to the Pickle."

"Wow, is this yours?"

"Yeah, why? Wanna drive it?"

"No, no, no. That's okay."

"Then get in. You're not one of those troglodytes who won't ride with a girl, are you?"

"Uh-uh."

"So let's get out of here."

"Out of school? I don't want to be counted absent."

"Oh, right. Cause then you'll turn up on 'America's Most Wanted'."

"Look, Jordan, I'm not goin' anywhere."

"Really? Well, you can't go back by yourself. Not without me. They'll think you killed me and hid my body in a culvert. Now, just move all that crap off the seat and get in."

I glanced inside: sketchbooks as big as cafeteria trays, pieces of lumber, part of a palm frond, bunches of half-dead mums, a hubcap, half a phone book, tubes of acrylic paint.

"And don't worry about detention or Saturday school," she said. "I'll fix everything tomorrow. The story is that you stayed pale and listless, so I had to drive you home and stay there until your mom showed up."

"What's Saturday school, anyway?"

"Punishment. Worse than detention, not as bad as suspension."

"Ms. Christophe burned some kid last Friday for vulgarity."

"Yeah, Ms. Christophe is very big on burning people for vulgarity."

Dumping stuff behind me, I settled in, pointing at something on the floor that was hairy, flat, and had six legs. "What's that?"

"The perfect road pizza. Part skunk, part raccoon. I guess

they got clipped together, creating the skunkoon—a portmanteau beast. I had my eye on it for days. Picked it up at just the right time."

I inched away from it, closer to the door. "Picked it up for what?"

"You never know." She reached across me, her ribs banging into my thighs, and tugged at the grotesque hide. "What if I only use these three hairs?" She brandished them. "The energy of the whole disaster is all in here if I want it."

I pushed her hand away from my face. "Okay, okay. I believe you."

As we lurched away from the parking lot, I asked if she had a driver's license.

"Of course. A brand-new one. I was sixteen two weeks ago."

"So how come you're only in tenth grade?"

"Missed a bunch of school along the way. Showed up here in the middle of the semester. Stuff like that."

We rode for a block or so before I said, "Day one, Barry terrorizes me. Day two, I get knocked out and then I get kidnapped. I can hardly wait for tomorrow."

"Barry's a jerk, but a very representative jerk."

"Meaning?"

"Meaning when he was throwing coupons all over the ground this morning so he could watch girls bend over, I kind of got an idea for a piece."

I pointed to a red light we were bearing down on. "Speaking of pieces, how about stopping or pieces of us will be all over the road." Then, looking both ways, I asked, "Is that what you were writing down this morning?"

"You saw that? Good for you. And, yeah, that's 'cause inspiration doesn't like to be neglected."

I watched her turn left, then right. I pointed to a realtor's sign with all its zeros. "How come even the little houses here cost a fortune?"

"The schools are good, and you can walk your dog at night without getting hit on the head by some crack addict."

"My aunt told my mom you can leave your door unlocked at night."

"I wouldn't go that far."

"But Hector said you can get brain-dead living here."

"That's true, too. There's a lot of flatliners roaming the streets and talking about where to get the best croissants."

Just then, somebody who passed us the other way honked and waved.

"Who was that?" I asked.

Jordan shrugged. "People know the Pickle." She turned left, then asked, "Was it nice where you came from before?"

"In Daly City? We lived in this, you know, tract house. Our neighbors were okay, I guess. It was crowded."

"Crowded?"

"People had a lot of stuff. Everybody bought a camper and then a boat and then an ATV."

"You went roaring around, tearing up the environment?"

I shook my head. "But we lived around guys who did. And it was all pretty new. The subdivision was called Stately Oaks, but the trees were all about three feet tall and they weren't even oaks." I looked out the window. "Compared to that, it's like West Paradise has been here forever."

"I like it that you noticed those trees."

"Why?"

"It just means you've got a good eye. Not everybody does." Then she zoomed toward the curb, skidded to a stop, and like somebody in a sitcom crowed, "Honey, I'm home."

"How did you know where I lived?"

"Hector and I found out. We drove by last night. Man,"

she said, leaning over me to take it all in, "is this ugly. Let's go in."

"If you think it's so ugly, what do you want to come in for?"

"Ugly's ugly, but that doesn't mean ugly isn't interesting." She bounced out of the car and barged up the walk. "Anyway, you owe me. I got you out of class."

I joined her on the porch. "Hey, you made me miss class."

"Whatever." She put her hand on the knob.

"Look, Jordan, I can't ask you to come in."

"Why not?"

"Um, my mom's sick."

"Really? What with? Is it contagious?"

"Well, actually, she's sad."

"Not sick."

I shook my head.

"Just sad."

I nodded.

"And *you* don't want me to see her sad, or *she* doesn't want me to see her sad."

"Well, I mean . . ."

Jordan put her ear to the door. "Maybe she went out. I don't hear anything."

"Sad people are quiet."

"When my dad is sad, he sobs. I don't hear any sobbing."

"She's past that part."

"So she what—whimpers?"

"She doesn't make any sounds, okay? She's just sad."

"Why?"

"Her husband died."

"This morning?"

"No!"

"And you said 'her husband,' not 'my father.' "

"Stepfather." I looked down at the ground. "My third."

"You're kidding. You had three stepfathers and a real dad before that?"

"Well, sure."

"And they all died?"

"Uh-huh."

"Jeez, you're not a kid, you're a collage." She shook her head. "Four dads. That's about one stormy moor and a couple of witches away from Shakespeare." She looked me up and down, frowning like I was the last Christmas tree on the lot.

"Whose name is Candelaria?"

"Dad's. I mean my real dad's."

"So when your mom got married again, she didn't change her—"

"She tried, but it got complicated."

"So what was your first stepfather's name?"

I looked down at my shoes. "Dennis De Boom."

"Making her Candelaria-De Boom. Sounds like a stripper."

"But she didn't use his—"

"And husband number three?"

"What's the difference, Jordan?"

"Better tell me, or I'll just nag you until you do."

"Kidder, okay? Russ Kidder."

"Candelaria-De Boom-Kidder. Interesting rhythm. And what's behind door number four?"

I sighed. "Bill Katt."

"Kidder-Katt. De Boom-Kidder-Katt. Candelaria-De Boom—"

"I know. I know. I've done it a thousand times. The point is that Candelaria is easier for both of us."

Jordan shook her head. "Hector's right. You've got secrets. Talking to you is like looking at the Pacific off Point Dread. What's down there, I wonder. How many wrecks? How much treasure?" She put her ear against the door again. "I think she went out."

"She never goes out by herself."

"She's out now."

"How do you know?"

"Open the door. Let's check."

"Are you nuts? What if she's home?"

"I say hello, I say I drove you home because you had a little accident but you're fine now, I say good-bye. 'Cause she's not going to believe you all by your lonesome when you try to explain why you're not in school. She's going to at least call Mr. Emery Board, right? And if she's not home, I get to see your astonishingly ugly condominium."

She wasn't going to let up, so I fished for my key. Well, it wouldn't hurt to give Mom a look at paint-splattered, Dr. Marten-wearing, motor-mouth Jordan. Then maybe she wouldn't think artists are so "interesting."

I turned the knob. "Just 'Hi, Tony's fine, good-bye,' right?"

She fanned herself with one hand. "Right."

I hurried ahead. "Mom?" Not in the kitchen. I backtracked and called upstairs, then glanced down into the den. Nothing.

"Food shopping?" Jordan ventured.

I shook my head. "I go food shopping."

"Yeah, right. For camp baloney."

"*Camarónes*. Let me look around."

I shot up the carpeted stairs before Jordan beat me to it. Mom's bed was made, and she wasn't in the bathroom. Downstairs, Jordan stood by the tile-covered counter we used as a table.

"So?"

"Wait a minute. I just remembered. She went to look for

a job. Which is good. This is only the second time she's been out on her own since Bill died."

"Bill the most recent stepdad?"

"Right."

Jordan sat down on the couch beside me, looked me right in the eye. "When my mom died, Dad bought a camper and we just drove around in circles." Suddenly she stood up, marched across the room and right into the downstairs bath, leaving the door open.

"Your mom died?" I asked.

"Yeah. She goes in for her annual physical, Dr. Mann finds a little spot on her lung. Four months later, she's gone."

I heard the light click on and, a few seconds later, off. Then she sat down beside me again.

"My teeth look like crap," she said. "Yours are gorgeous. What do you brush with, uranium?"

"Rembrandt, but tell me about your—"

"The dead painter?"

"It's a kind of toothpaste." I scooted closer. "Tell me what happened after your mom died. You were driving around with your father, and . . .?"

"Oh, yeah. Well, I skipped the part where he got really sick and almost bought the farm. It was after that we took to the open road. Or because of that."

"What'd he get sick from?"

She shrugged, looked down at her chewed-up fingernails. "Grief. Broken heart. He loved my mom a lot." Jordan tried to push her stubborn hair back. "Me, too." Suddenly she shot to her feet. "Can I have a Coke?"

"Uh, there's just bottled water."

She nodded, headed for the refrigerator. "Wow," she exclaimed, looking inside. "This must be where good Tupperware goes when it dies."

I walked over to the counter. "So your dad got sick and fled?"

She nodded as she twisted the cap off a bottle of Crystal Geyser. "Nice verb. Fled is exactly what he did. He fled from one health joint to another—the Ozarks, Sante Fe, Sedona. Crystal therapy, hot pools at Satan's Springs, deep tissue massage, juice fasting—you name it, he tried it. Finally, though, a few years ago we landed here and Dad went back to work."

"Doing what?"

"Painting. As in artist, not house. He's Drew Archer." I must have looked blank. "Your line is, 'Not *the* Drew Archer.'"

"Sorry."

"That's okay. He's pretty famous, though, as those things go."

"How long did it take him to get over your mom dying and all?"

She shook her head. "I'm not sure he ever really got over it. But he paints, anyway. And, you know, I have my art, too."

I leaned across the counter. "Man, I wish my mom would paint or work or something."

"You must hate her sometimes."

That made me squirm. "My mom? God, no."

"Hey, it's okay to hate your mother. Everybody does it."

"Not me."

"So that's not a secret you want to share with me right now. That's cool."

I didn't know what to say, so I pointed to her bottled water. When she shook her head, I walked over to the little refrigerator Mom kept by the desk. I wrapped one hand around a cool bottle of Crystal Geyser and just held it. "I don't have any secrets."

54

"Right, Mr. Four Dads. And I'm up for Playmate of the Year."

"I don't."

"Tony, I'm not just nosy—understand that. And I'm not doing walk-in therapy like our beloved guidance counselor, Mr. Passmore Gas. I want to know more about you 'cause I'm into the aesthetics of concealment. And you—man, it looks to me like you have got to have a dark side and a half." She pulled me down on the couch beside her. "Here's the deal. I told you a secret; now you tell me a secret. Then we're even."

"I told you, I don't have any—"

"Oh, please. One lousy little secret from what has to be a dank, serpent-ridden shadow world."

She caught me glancing toward the den. "What? What's down there? Some hideous laboratory? Freddy Krueger's rec room?"

"About an hour ago, you said if I danced with you you'd never bother me again."

"I said I wouldn't bother you about *dancing*. This is different. But the deal's the same—one secret, and you're off the hook."

"Forever?"

"Forever."

I looked at her, inspected her actually. "And no more blackmail."

"Right, right. Now what's downstairs? It's not a freezer, is it, with all those dads intact?"

"God, no! It's just a tape. For a VCR."

She sprang to her feet. "Yes! Ready-to-wear media. Perfect."

"But this is between you and me."

"Fine. I won't tell, but I might use it in a piece."

"What? Why?"

"Because I might use anything in a piece. I want to die in a gallery, okay? I've already got that installation half-worked out in my head. And if I'm willing to use my own demise, I figure it's okay to use just about anything anybody tells me." She reached for my hand again. "I'll promise this much—it'll end up so transformed that nobody'll ever know."

I took a step back. "This isn't a good idea."

"Look," she said, sounding serious all of a sudden. "I have to see this, Tony. I *have* to."

"Why?"

"You remember what Rochelle said at school the other day, how Blue wins prizes and Hector has stuff under consideration and all I do is talk?"

"She was mad."

"She was right. Or at least it looks that way."

"You were just late to that art show. Blue said that Barbie thing was good."

"But I'm always late or I don't finish or I get sick." Her cheeks were burning as she plunged ahead. "I don't draw very well, okay? And I'm only a so-so painter. I'm not strong enough to sculpt; Dad let me try it and I about broke my foot."

She took a deep breath. "I want to work with images of sound now; I *am* working with them. And anything that I can see or hear in that area is going to be good for me and expand my creativity. So if there's some killer video, let me look at it. Please. Nobody's going to know." When she grabbed my hands, hers were ice cold.

"What if Mom comes home?"

"What about it?"

"What are we doing down there?"

"Watching a video."

56

"She's not supposed to know that!"

"Not the secret video. *A* video."

I nodded. "Okay. But don't tell her why I'm home early. I don't want her to know I was dancing."

"Why, is she Amish?"

"Just say I ate some bad cafeteria food, okay? She'll understand that."

"Hey, if you want, I'll say you got too many *A*'s and were sent home before you undermined the self-esteem of everybody in the tenth grade. I just want one look at this tape."

"Well," I said finally. "Come on."

Jordan was actually rubbing her hands together as she followed me down carpeted stairs into the den.

"This is so great!" she said.

I went straight to the VCR as she looked around, taking in the subterranean walls—with damp spots showing through—and the tiny ground-level windows that were narrow as silverware drawers.

"Wow," she said. "A tomb with a view." Then she added, "Where's the other video, in case suspicious old Mom comes in."

"Oh, yeah." I picked one off the shelf.

Jordan looked at it. "*The Art of Sensual Massage*? This is going to be okay with her?"

I blushed and grabbed for it. "I didn't buy that." I handed her another one.

"*The Lion King*, huh."

"Mom says the songs make her feel better."

"Hey, when massage isn't enough, go for the singing baboon."

I pushed buttons and stepped back. "Mom still watches this. But she doesn't know that I know she still watches it.

So it's her secret, too. You get two for one." I squatted back down again and fiddled with the tracking knob. "And she just can't keep watching it and watching it. We've got to move on."

Jordan was staring at me. I could feel it. "Well," she said slowly, "there's moving on like in pack up the boxes and call the van, and there's moving on. Which one are we talking about here?"

I hit the play button hard, and on came the video. That video. The one a neighbor had shot on Bill's birthday. The quality wasn't that good, but then it'd been played a lot.

I just turned my back. I didn't have to see it again. The sound track told me everything: "You put your left foot in," everyone sang, "you put your left foot out."

I walked over and squatted down in front of one of the boxes we hadn't unpacked. Sitting right on top was the basketball Bill and I used to play with.

I knew the camera was zooming in on Billy, the birthday boy. I dribbled a few times, bounced the ball off the wall at an angle so it was like a bad pass, and scooped it up smoothly anyway.

About now Bill was clutching his chest. His mouth opened and closed like those poor trout on fishing shows. Then he looked for Mom. Then he toppled over.

He'd showed me how to do that thing where you spin the ball and balance it on one finger. So I did that, did it well, too. But Bill wasn't there to tell me how good that looked, or to try and knock it away while I blocked him out. I let the ball drop back into the box.

Jordan came up behind me. "You okay?"

I took a deep breath. "Sure, why?"

"You're standing in the corner."

I turned around. "I've seen it before, that's all."

"Did he have a heart attack? He looks like he was in great shape."

"He was, but the doctor said afterward it was something that wouldn't show up on a test until it was too late, so . . ."

"Who shot that film, anyway?"

"We don't know. Four or five people at the party took turns with Mom's camcorder." I shook my head and sighed.

Jordan sat down beside me. "Whoever did it showed a lot of composure. I mean, he can see your dad's—"

I corrected her. "Stepdad."

"—your stepdad's in trouble, but instead of helping him he cranks in for a close-up." Jordan guzzled some water, then wiped her mouth. "My dad says that artists are the most callous people in the world 'cause we use everything in our work. *Everything.*" She handed me the Crystal Geyser.

The bottle was warm where her hand had been. The top, too.

"Are you that way?" I asked. "Callous, I mean?"

She picked up the remote and hit rewind. "Can I make a copy of that?"

"I guess that answers my question."

"I'd ask your mom first."

"That isn't a good idea."

"Just for the record, what's your mother's name?"

"Kate. Kathryn."

She shook her head. "Kate drinks beer, likes Stove Top stuffing, and wears tight jeans. Kathryn lies on the couch in a peignoir, a lavender-scented cloth on her forehead. Which is it?"

"I call her Mom. Who calls their mother by her first name?"

"Barry calls his mom Sheila. And Hector's mother wants everybody to call her Lupe."

"It's still weird."

"You should try calling your mom Kathryn and see what happens."

"No, thanks."

"Are you afraid of new experiences?"

"I'm talking to you, aren't I?"

She rubbed her hands together. "I want to spend some time with Kathryn, okay? She sounds interesting."

"I showed you the tape. You said we were even."

"This isn't just about me." She scratched her head, then scowled at her fingernails. "I got it! We take her to the Dada show."

"Dada?"

"Not as in Mama, and not—in your case—Stepdada. But as in the Dada movement, as in surrealism. Dad and I go every year; we'll just add you two."

"I don't think so."

"Do you want her to get better faster?"

"No art show is going to do that."

"Not the art show itself. But going to the art show might."

"Going?"

"Sure. Remember what I told you about my dad, how sad and screwed up he was after Mom died?"

"Yeah, so?"

"So he didn't really get better until he started going places."

"I thought you said all you did was drive around to different health joints and stuff?"

"We did, then he'd stay inside and sob into this magic Peruvian mud. But when I got him off his butt and out into the real world, he got better."

"So this is an unselfish act on your part, right? It's all for Mom?"

"I get to meet her, sure. I get to talk to her and listen to her. And maybe I can use something she says, some special little Kathryn-rhythm. But so what? Basically, we'll just have a good time."

"I don't think so, Jordan," I said.

"So Saturday, okay?" She slid past me and I followed her up the last couple of stairs. "Tell your mom. Don't ask her, tell her. And don't worry." She opened the front door and stepped outside. "Everything will be fine."

Stunned, I waved good-bye, then wandered back in and looked out the window where Jordan was just pulling away from the curb. Man, she was something. But *what* was she, that was the question.

I glanced at the phone. Nah, what good would talking to Confess-O-Rama do. I looked in the fridge instead, cut off a little slice of cheese, and ate it. I glanced at the phone again.

Then I picked a plastic daisy out of its vase and played I call you/I call you not, working my way around the stiff petals.

Okay, fine. I wouldn't call. I'd do the dishes.

That took about two minutes. I wiped the sink clean with a sponge. I folded the little yellow towel and hung it up.

"Oh, just call," I said out loud. "What's it going to hurt? Who's going to know."

I leaned against the wall, listened to the message. "Hi," I said. "It's me again. I just had this weird experience. Do you remember that girl I told you about last time? The one who gets on everybody's nerves? Well, I just spent about two hours with her."

I carried the phone to the sink, drank a little water right from the faucet like a dog, wiped my mouth on my T-shirt.

"I mean this when I say there's only one word for her—relentless. She never gives up. She says dance, I say no, I end up dancing. She says show me something, I say no, I end up showing her something."

61

I turned in a tight circle, winding myself in the phone cord, then unwinding like a huge mobile.

"But I'm going out with her. Wait, I mean *I'm* not going out with her. She's not the kind of girl I'd ever go on a date with. Can't you just see her at the prom with her road pizza wrist corsage and turpentine behind her ears? Mom and I are going out with her and her dad, that's all. Which is probably a good idea, actually. And even if it's not, we're going anyway 'cause I haven't found the stop button for Jordan."

I listened to the hiss of the machine, which didn't care if I went on or not. I got another drink. I wound myself up again.

"Oh, guess what? Her mom died. And she moved around a lot. So even though we're completely different, we're a little bit alike. Isn't *that* weird."

Then I got a look at myself in the kitchen window: one fifteen-year-old boy with a sweaty phone in his hand talking seriously *to a machine*!

"I gotta go," I said. When I hung up, I just slid to the floor and stayed there.

By Saturday afternoon I was pretty nervous, so I got into the cupboard and took down my green jars full of lentils, peas, and garbanzo beans.

They looked gorgeous standing there on the blue tile, and they felt great as I measured out a couple of handfuls each, letting them trickle through my fingers and into the stainless steel bowl.

I raked through again, turning them over like pirates are supposed to fondle doubloons and pieces of eight. With my free hand I reached for the radio.

"So censorship is fine until somebody tries to censor you. Is that what you're saying?"

Larry Deluxe. I twirled the knob, settling on R.E.M. just as Mom came through the front door, closed it behind her, and leaned on it. She dabbed at her eyes with a Kleenex.

"It's a harsher world than I remember," she said.

"You weren't gone very long."

"They said no—one of the shortest words in the English language."

I ran water into the bowl and shook a couple of bay leaves

in; they circled each other like the *Monitor* and the *Merrimac*. I looked in my refrigerator for the things I would need later: onions, carrots, tomatoes, garlic. "What kind of job was it this time?"

Mom dabbed at her eyes. "Oh, just hostess at The Salt Cellar down the street." She straightened up, tucking her white blouse into brown linen pants. "The manager said I was attractive . . ."

"You are attractive," I said automatically.

"But . . ."

"C'mon." I closed the refrigerator door and leaned against it. "Wash your face. They'll be here pretty soon."

"Oh, Lord. I'd much rather take off my shoes, lie on the couch, and watch *The Lion King*."

"You've been watching *The Lion King* all week."

"Tony, I went out today!"

"For forty-five minutes." I walked toward her. "Look, I know we're not going to settle here, but that doesn't mean we have to act like hermits. Think of it as practice for when we move back east."

"It all seems so pointless."

"See, you're depressed again. You need to get out."

"I don't want to be around a lot of married people today."

"It's an art show. Artists don't get married; it's too conventional."

"On the other hand, I don't want to be around a lot of desperate singles, either."

"It's an art show. All artists are married; it's called a collaboration."

She laughed in spite of herself. "I suppose it wouldn't hurt to spend a quiet afternoon in a gallery with two knowledgeable people."

"Exactly!"

"Not that it matters, but what's this Drew Archer like?"

"I haven't met him, but Jordan is . . . let's say unusual."

"That probably means he's unusual, too. He's not like that Elephant Man, is he?"

"Well, okay, I admit it: I hear he paints with his trunk."

She sighed, then tossed her Kleenex in the wastebasket. "She paints, too, is that what you said?"

I walked across the room, peeked out the miniblinds. "I said she'd tried painting, but she's sort of into images now or sound or something. I know she used to do these pieces, though."

"Pizzas?"

"Yeah, Mom, right. She's a pizza artist. 'We deliver culture to your home in thirty minutes or you don't pay.' I said *pieces*."

"What are pieces?"

"Well, the only one I really know about is this . . ." Dead Barbie. "Uh, this one she could've won a prize for."

"Could have?"

"She was, uh, late for the, you know, show."

"So she's not pretty and she's chronically late."

"That's right, make her sound like an old bus."

"This isn't someone you're interested in, is it?"

"Mom, she was nice enough to invite us to go with—"

"I understand."

"Good."

She walked to the downstairs bathroom and peered into the mirror over the sink. "I certainly look forty-two," she declared.

Mom stepped back into the living room. She took in my fresh-from-the-cleaners slacks and white shirt. "You look nice."

"Jordan said people get dressed up for this, so . . ."

"Do you think I should change?"

"You look fine." Just then I heard a car horn outside.

"Couldn't they come to the door instead of honking. We're not geese."

"Speak for yourself. I feel like flying south for the winter." I was headed for the window again when the doorbell rang.

"It's them." I opened the door. *Oh, my God.*

I closed the door. "It wasn't them."

Mom looked puzzled. "Then who was it?"

"I don't know."

"Well, look."

When I opened the door again, there stood a guy in khakis and a faded denim shirt. "I'm Drew Archer."

I shook his hand. "Uh, where'd Jordan go?"

"Right here!" She jumped out from behind him wearing jeans, a T-shirt, and—outside of that, over it—something electric. Something that flashed: green on the left, red on the right.

I tried to keep my eyes up, on her cocky grin or her slicked-back hair. Oh, no, I thought, turning to watch my mother take Jordan in. One eye started to twitch. Her left arm came up across her chest like she was saluting somebody from Mars.

"Guys are always so interested in girls' underwear," Jordan explained without being asked, "so I thought I'd just clear up that sexist mystery." She raised both hands. "Here it is. Now what?" She looked at me. "Remember Barry the other day ogling that girl in the crop top?"

I managed to grunt, "Uh-huh."

"Now nobody has to try to sneak a peek, and there's no more mixed signals on the sexual expressway: red means stop, green means go." Then she tugged at her father. "C'mon. Look at their refrigerator."

"Do you mind?" asked Drew Archer, nodding to my mother.

"My refrigerator? No, I guess not," she sputtered.

They divided Mom and me and, when they'd passed, she gave me one of those glances that equal what can be packed into a microchip. Then she slipped up beside me. "Tony, she's wearing an electric bra!"

"She is? I didn't notice." Then I took hold of Mom's arm, but it was hard to tell who was holding who up.

Once the two of them had peered into the big, double-doored Amana, Drew Archer walked back into the living room and scoped everything out: the heavy cotton drapes, the green carpet, my aunt's furniture, and—last but not least—Mom.

"Jordan," he said, looking at me, "thought I might like to paint it."

"My mother?" I blurted.

He laughed easily. "No, the refrigerator. And I might. There's something I like about it's austere organization."

"Tony loves Tupperware," Jordan quipped. "I saw it written on the wall in the girls' bathroom."

"C'mon," I said, ducking my head and heading for the door. "Let's get out of here."

We settled into a new Saturn station wagon. It was spotless inside and out, the complete opposite of Jordan's Honda. Drew Archer drove carefully for a block or two. Then at the first stop light Jordan turned so she could kneel in the front seat and face my mother and me. Her bra blinked at us: stop go stop go.

I stared at the back of the seat.

"So?" Jordan said jauntily, "whaddaya been up to, Kathryn?"

I felt Mom stiffen. She stared at the flashing lights. "Well," she said as we turned onto Seca Street, "I've been looking for a job."

"Do you need the money?" Jordan asked.

Mom flinched again. "For the moment."

"Well, it could've been just for distraction, right? To take your mind off all those husbands."

Mom swiveled in her seat and stared out the window.

I glared at Jordan, who looked back wide-eyed and mouthed, "What?"

Her father's hand drifted off the steering wheel and across her mouth. "Jordan, give Mrs. Candelaria a little room to breathe. She's not used to your fabled directness."

"But, Dad, you'll love this: she marries four guys and they all die."

Drew Archer took his foot off the gas and we coasted. "Surely not."

"Dead as doornails," said Jordan.

His knuckles went white on the steering wheel as the station wagon picked up speed. "Dead," he murmured. "All four."

As Mom clutched my wrist, he dodged a minivan and weaved in and out of traffic.

"Listen, everybody," he announced. "It's right on the way. Just a quick stop. No problem." But he didn't sound convinced; in fact, he sounded like a flight attendant telling us to sit back and relax as the plane plummeted toward earth.

He hung a wide U-turn, powered up a driveway, and skidded to a halt in front of Wong's Health Foods. The Saturn lurched a little as he shoved it into park and got out. He tugged at his belt. He fiddled with his button-down collar.

"Just a little errand," he explained. "No time at all. On our way in a jiffy."

Jordan climbed out, adjusted her bra, and ambled around to Mom's side of the car.

My mother hissed, "What's wrong with him? We could have been killed."

"Mom, how do I . . .?"

"And what's wrong with her? That thing she's got on. She's flashing!"

The back door swung open. "C'mon, you guys," Jordan urged. "He'll be okay in a minute."

Mom clicked on her smile, held out one hand, and stepped out gracefully.

I looked around. I recognized the Arco station across the street and the car wash catercornered from us but not the low little building we were parked in front of.

"Everybody who works here is named Wong," Jordan explained as we filed toward the door. "So the family joke is that it's all Wong, but that's all wight."

The glass door was plastered with pictures of people doing yoga and machines that could get juice out of everything but rocks. I held it open as Jordan tugged at my other arm. "Say hi to Mrs. Wong and Art and his wife, June."

I shook their hands, then pulled Jordan aside. "What happened to your dad?" I whispered.

"He just has to make sure he's not dead. C'mon, let's get something to drink."

As Jordan opened the tall glass door, I saw Mrs. Wong touch my mother's arm and say something. Mom was about five eight anyway, but she was so pulled together, she looked closer to six feet.

"She's upset."

"So?" Jordan nudged me with an open pint of orange juice. "Drink some. I don't have germs or if I do, they're good germs, smart germs, the Galileo and Mozart of germs. Germs that—"

"What have you been smoking?" I asked, inching away.

She shook her head. "Nothing. I've been up since six working and it went really well, so I'm stoked. How about you. You look a little stressed."

I scanned green moss for your face, cans of something called brewer's yeast, a bin of organic oranges that looked like cat toys. I looked anywhere and everywhere but at those lights. But finally I couldn't help myself.

I pointed to her neon bra. "What's with this?"

She stuck out her nonexistent chest proudly. "I wanted to get dressed up for the Dada show."

"Dressed up? Neon underwear is not getting dressed up." I pointed to myself. "This is dressed up."

"You look nice, too. Anonymous in a kind of weekend way."

"My mom about died when she saw your outfit."

Jordan glanced toward the counter where Mom was pretending to look at vitamins. "She looks okay to me. Are you sure you don't mean that *you* almost died when you saw my outfit?"

I watched her shirt turn red, then green. I felt my face turn red, then redder. "You aren't embarrassed, even a little?"

Jordan licked her lips while she thought it over. "Oh, somewhere down there, probably, cause I've been socialized like everybody else. But you can't be a good artist and pay attention to stuff like that. And I don't want to come off sounding too political standing here among the loofah pads and Sea of Galilee Bowel Invigorator, but being embarrassed and making nice and always smelling good are some man's idea of what a woman should be." Then she turned red, like her right boob, and looked down at her ratty shoes. "End of speech."

"So you're not just chronically weird."

"Oh, that, too. I hope, anyway." She looked over one shoulder, then held out one hand. "C'mon. Speaking of weird, this is worth seeing."

At the back of the store, Drew Archer perched beside a card table. Mr. Wong sat behind it, his back to a wall decorated with outlines of men, lines running everywhere on their bodies.

Her dad's hand lay on a tiny pillow, and Mr. Wong—his eyes almost closed—pressed one finger, then another, then another along Drew's wrist.

Just then Mr. Wong took a deep breath, let it out, and said, "Don't worry, Drew Archer. Your pulses are very strong."

Jordan's dad stood up, smiling. "Do Kathryn," he said.

Mom kept her arms crossed like she was guarding a vault. "Are you sure? Aren't you worried I might be too toxic to touch?"

Drew Archer cradled her elbow, and she inched toward the chair. "I apologize for my behavior," he said smoothly. "I'm a little sensitive when it comes to health issues."

I watched Mr. Wong's fingers—the same three a trumpet player uses—press on Mom's wrist. I watched him frown.

"Much sorrow," he said finally.

"Now she'll cry," I murmured.

Mom sniffed and reached for a Kleenex.

"Lungs are weeping." Then Mr. Wong wrote down two or three things on a piece of paper and handed them to her. "Herbs will help."

When Mom glanced up at Drew, he smiled and said, "They can't hurt."

Mr. Wong looked Jordan over, scanned her almost. "Need

batteries for bosom lights?" he asked. "Or run off own energy?"

Jordan worked up a grin. "I've got a battery pack in here somewhere." Then she linked her arm through her dad's, and they all trooped toward the front of the store.

Mr. Wong eyed the bin I was inspecting. He had some interesting stuff: black turtle beans, adzuki beans, quinoa.

"Do you know these?" he asked in what was almost a whisper.

"No. I've heard of them, though. In cookbooks."

"Ah, you cook."

"I know how."

Mr. Wong opened a plastic lid and invited me to take some.

"Drew Archer likes these," he said.

"Jordan eats mung beans?"

"No, Jordan eats what you call Pop-Tarts."

"They don't eat together?"

He shook his head. "Do not even live together. You have not seen duplex? Perfect polarities—yin and yang, male and female, hot and cold, intellect and intuition." He reached for a plastic bag. "I give you some. Fix them, tell me what you think."

"No, really."

"I insist." He reached for an aluminum scoop. "Friends of Jordan and Drew Archer are friends of Wong."

We joined the others at the counter, where Mrs. Wong was ringing things up. "Do not even live together." I couldn't believe it.

Mom turned to me and asked for twenty dollars. "I don't like to think of my lungs weeping."

Jordan watched me open my wallet and hand over the

money. She drifted away and I followed. She looked at the spotless floor. I read a sign that promised POTENCY FOR MEN.

Finally I blurted, "I'm sorry I was mad before. I worry about my mom."

She smiled at me. "That's okay. No harm, no foul."

"Really? That's it?"

"Sure."

"When we fight at Casa Candelaria, it can go on for days."

"Hey, you apologized. I accepted. It's over." She grinned a little. "Right?"

"Cool."

"So, what are we waiting for? Let's go see some art." Her hand slid up my arm and settled on my biceps; I flexed so she wouldn't feel a sleeveful of tapioca.

"Guys?" called Drew Archer. "Ready?"

Mrs. Wong and June hugged Drew Archer. Art and Mr. Wong shook his hand, holding it a long time with both of theirs.

A minute later we settled into the Saturn, this time with the alleged grown-ups in the front.

"The Wongs," Mom said, "are very nice people."

Drew Archer just nodded as he carefully changed lanes on the winding freeway that led into downtown.

"How," Mom asked, "did you get interested in alternative medicine?"

"When my wife died," he explained, "I apparently tried to die, too. I only got about halfway, though." I could see his clear blue eyes in the mirror as he added, "And I promise not to swerve into the retaining wall if you tell us about your husbands."

Jordan leaned forward. Her eyes were almost as bright as the lights on her boobs. "What were their names?" she asked.

"Manuel, Dennis, Russ, and Bill." She left big tombstone-size spaces between each one. I expected Jordan to smirk, but she didn't. She just asked, "Manuel was Tony's father?"

Mom nodded. "So gorgeous."

"And Dennis?"

"Vigorous, robust."

"Where did you guys live?" Drew asked from the front seat.

"In Washington. I was modeling at a boat show; that's where I met Dennis."

"But he was a pilot on the Mississippi," I said, "like Mark Twain. So we had to move to St. Louis."

"And Russ?" Jordan asked.

"Burly, fun-loving, talented."

"That's when we moved to Tucson," I said.

"He wrote *Apache Tears, Apache Trails, Apache Terrors*—"

"I bought a couple of those books once 'cause the covers were so cool," said Jordan. "But when I tried to read 'em, the same Native American detective was solving the same mystery every time."

"I'm sure *your* work sells in the tens of thousands." Mom sounded icy.

"Well, not yet."

I liked the way she could do that—just say anything she wanted, and the insults or irony slipped off her like she wore Teflon.

"How about Bill?" Jordan asked.

"Steady," Mom stated. "Dependable, honest."

Jordan nodded approvingly. "Nice lists."

"Thank you, I'm sure."

Jordan was like those snapping turtles; even when the sun went down, she wouldn't give up. "How did they die?"

Mom glanced at Drew Archer, probably expecting him to

warn his daughter again. But he just looked over and smiled a little like he wanted to know, too.

"Well, Dad was shot during a coup, Dennis drowned, Russ fell off a cliff, and Bill had a heart attack."

"Wow," said Jordan. "It's like an anthology of demise." Then she whipped out a piece of paper and started to scribble and sketch.

Mom plunged one hand into her Wong's Health Foods bag, hauled out a squat-looking jar, and read—or pretended to read—the label.

Jordan slid back beside me. "What was that like?" she whispered. "Having all your dads die?"

"Are you kidding?" I scooted away from her. "I'm not going to talk to you about that."

"Why not?"

"I don't even know you."

"Sure, you do. This is me. What you see is what you get."

"Well, then, I don't trust you. I'm liable to tell you something and it'll end up in a painting."

"But that's exactly why you *can* trust me. You know I'll use it if I can, so it'll get changed. Secrets to me are like clay: they come looking one way, and then you make them into something else. So tell me." She pointed to her ear. "Whisper it. Start like this: When all my dads and stepdads died, I . . ."

"No way!"

"I can't imagine," Drew Archer said, "losing more than one person that you care about. I really admire your resilience, Kathryn."

"Well," Mom said, snapping and unsnapping her little gold purse, "I had Tony to consider and then to lean on." She reached back and patted my knee. "Without him I don't know . . ." She let the sentence hang.

"I didn't pay much attention to Jordan at all," Drew Archer said in a neutral tone.

"You're telling me. I had to walk myself to school holding my own hand."

"How old were you?" blurted my mother.

Jordan shrugged. "Eight or so."

"No wonder," Mom said under her breath.

Jordan reached around to scratch under the thick bra strap. "I'm still curious about that job you didn't get this morning. Where'd you look?"

"I interviewed at The Salt Cellar."

"Hostess," Jordan declared.

Mom looked back at her. "Why, yes."

"You're not the waitress type. Too elegant. So did you score?"

"Um, no." Mom took a hanky out of her hanky-size purse and blotted her forehead. "I was given an armful of menus, shown how to hold them . . ."

"You're kidding!" Jordan squirmed, loving it. "Lessons in menu holding!"

"Then sent to greet the next party. I was nervous, you understand, so I just looked at the gentleman's tie and said, 'Good morning. Would you like a table or a booth?' And just as he said, 'A booth, please,' I glanced up, saw how much he resembled Bill, and burst into tears."

Jordan cackled. "So did he say, 'A table will be fine'?"

Mom got stiff all over again as Drew Archer pointed and announced, "The Ironworks. We're almost there."

"And not a minute too soon," I said almost to myself. Then, taking in the big, rough-looking buildings, blurted, "What's the Ironworks? Hector was talking about it."

"It's Art City now," Jordan answered. "But it was a real ironworks once; then when that went belly up some developer bought it and turned it into studio space—you know, high ceilings, north light, the whole loft scene."

Drew took a sloping freeway ramp. As we swooped down into the city, huge flowers of graffiti blossomed on the walls around us. The homeless wandered with their carts and argued, usually with nobody.

"This is so different," Mom said, "from where we live."

"You should see West Paradise from the air," said Drew Archer. "It's a little oasis of green. I had somebody take me up so I could get some pictures for a project of mine. It's just what the name says it is—a paradise. We had our centennial last year and some of the trees are older than that."

Jordan began pointing. "While here we have cement as far as the eye can see and stately security gates. Still, they've got an art gallery, café, and a place to buy supplies. And there's nowhere to go, and nothing to do but work."

"And you and Hector and Blue were going to live here?"

"*Are* going to live here, the minute we get out of high school. We'll just get space for three instead of four. Unless you want to join us."

"Me? What would I do in an artists' colony?"

"What were you going to do wherever?"

"I don't know."

"You could do that here."

Drew switched off the ignition, reached into a side pocket on the car door, and took out two huge bananas. I could see Mom brace herself.

"Potassium," he explained, tossing one into the backseat, peeling the other deftly and handing half to my mom.

I was still staring at the one he'd given me when Jordan urged me to play along.

"Just do it, Cheetah. He won't let us out until you do."

So I peeled it, gave her half, put the yellow skin in Drew's outstretched hand, and we all sat there chewing until Drew unlocked the car door. Then he held up a small plastic bottle. "Bee pollen?"

"No," Jordan said. "We won't know whether to swing from the rafters or sting somebody. Now, c'mon."

I hopped out, circled the shiny station wagon, and joined Jordan. Drew Archer gulped God knows what; Mom sat there, her door open, looking gloomy.

In the west, a fat inner tube of smog had turned pink. Somewhere out there the sun was sinking toward the Pacific.

I knew what was going on with my mother because I'd seen it before. Lots of times. But Drew Archer knew, too. He figured it out. Or maybe remembered.

"Evening can be a sad time," he said.

Mom bit her lower lip, and I reached for my little package of Kleenex. The one I carried for her.

"I'll be fine in a minute," she said.

I watched Jordan study her.

Drew Archer leaned, said something, and Mom let herself be helped out. He stood beside her, patted one hand briskly, then tucked her arm in his.

"Ruskin started all that in *Modern Painters*," he said. "He claimed that the sky speaks to the human heart, 'soothing it,'" Drew quoted, "'and purifying it from its dross and dust.' Before that book, when the sun went down it probably was just time to go to bed."

Mom took a deep breath, then raised her head bravely. "It's hard to believe that the sunset didn't always make most people think of the ends of things."

"Remember when your mother was talking about your fathers?" whispered Jordan. "On the way down here, I mean. See if I've got her delivery right." She pointed to a red-haired guy coming toward us at an angle. "Bold," she whispered,

78

"impulsive, chivalric." She picked another one, wearing a shirt the color of exposed film. "Merciless, cursory." Then a third with a big ruffled collar, like kale: "Headlong, enterprising, Arcadian." She beamed at me, proud of herself.

I grinned back because she'd actually done pretty well. Mom talked that way, with those rat-a-tat-tat adjectives. Plus, *cursory* was a cool word. Also *chivalric.* You didn't run into that many kids with a good vocabulary anymore. Mine was as good as it was because when Mom was in bad shape, I'd sit up and read. Anyhow, I started to think that maybe Jordan wasn't as flaky as I'd thought.

When my mother waved, I walked over. She looked at the guys Jordan had just described and whispered, "Some of these people look dangerous." She leaned closer. "When we're not together, keep your eyes open. Don't talk to strangers."

"You sound like Officer Dog. I'll be fine."

"At least stay behind Jordan."

"Good idea. Maybe they'll shoot her first."

Jordan swooped down, hooked my arm with hers, and pulled me off the walk. "You guys go on. We'll find you later." Then to me, "What'd your mother want?"

I sighed. "To tell me the world's a dangerous place."

"I hope so. Otherwise, I'd be bored. Now, c'mon. Let's check out some of these studios."

When I didn't bolt right into the first one, she tugged hard and said, "Relax. I'll protect you."

I backed away. "You never stop, do you?"

"Not till I melt down." She reached for me. "Something you haven't seen yet, and not a pretty picture."

I was beginning to like the feel of her arm wound around mine, so I let her lead me, but I couldn't help glancing back. "That stuff about my dads and how they died and all could have been a three-Valium conversation. But look at my mom—she's fine."

"Hey, she's not china."

Really?

Jordan nudged me. "C'mon now. I won't talk about my art if you won't talk about your mom. Deal?"

I took her hand and shook it. "Deal."

I started to check out the other people, some of them not much older than Jordan or me. Almost all the guys, I noticed, had ponytails. All of them were also too cool or too weird to give Jordan's bra more than a passing glance. Or maybe they'd got used to stuff like this.

"Sure I can get in these studios with this normal hair?" I asked.

"We'll say you just got out of rehab. In Utah."

Inside the first place, things were spick-and-span or at least as spick-and-span as concrete could be. On the nearest wall hung a picture of a woman on a crucifix. At her feet three bald white men in suits played cards.

"This hasn't got a title," I said.

"Oh, it's . . . you know—oppression by the patriarchal culture. That's all Barbara ever paints."

"Are they all like this?" I asked.

"Political? Probably. More or less."

"So I should stop looking for a painting of two stallions fighting on a mountain while a storm rages."

"That might be a good idea."

"And no bowls of fruit."

"Nope."

She led me toward the huge glass window at the far end of the loft. We stopped there and looked out. I could see the other sheds and storage units that'd been turned into what Jordan called space. The sun bounced off their huge windows.

She took the toe of her hiking boot and traced some of the paint that'd been spilled on the floor. "I'm not nuts about Barbara's politics, but she really works hard. I like people who work."

"That lets me out."

"Hey, the way I read it, your mom's a full-time job." Then she tugged me toward an orange couch that looked like a geometry problem. "We forgot. We wouldn't talk about art or moms."

"Right."

"So no more, okay?"

"Okay."

We just sat there for a minute or so until Jordan sighed.

"What?" I asked.

"I'm just anxious to live down here and really get some work done."

"And I was just thinking how cool it'd be to live anywhere without my mother."

"Maybe we should agree to talk about nothing *but* art and moms."

We stood up, grinning, and I followed Jordan as she sliced between a couple of out-of-season leather jackets at the door. Outside the light was tired-looking.

We had to step aside to let three girls in black glide by. One smiled at me. I looked at the ground. Actually, I *studied* the ground like I had to write an essay about it.

"You're shy with girls, aren't you," Jordan asked.

"Jordan, she was wearing a skull with little red eyes. In her nose."

I thought what a nice laugh she had.

She caught me thinking. "What?" she asked.

"Nothing."

"C'mon. What?"

"You should use yourself for your art thing. Your laugh, I mean."

She ducked her head and tugged at my hand. "C'mon. One more loft, then we'll hit the big gallery."

The open door was guarded by a mannequin wearing camouflage pants and a camouflage crop top. The closer we got, the more I could hear whistles, explosions, and chattering machine guns.

Jordan knelt right in front of the one-armed dummy. "There's a little TV in her tummy," she announced. "Want to check it out?"

I took a step backward. "Call me old-fashioned, but I don't want to watch war movies through somebody's navel."

Jordan held one hand out and I helped her up. "It's the same old sex and violence loop, anyway."

We stepped through another door together. There was nothing inside except a bed standing exactly in the center of this long room. Black silk sheets were pulled so tight the top one reflected the last of the light angling in through the big north window. An easel held one white card, which said *Rendering the Familiar Strange*.

I looked at it from a couple of sides. "It's a bed! Do artists get paid for this?

"Not right away. Mostly you just show as much as you can to expand your portfolio. Then you trot that into some big gallery and maybe they'll look at your new stuff."

I pointed. "So the portfolio doesn't say, 'I was a good boy and made my bed.' It says *Rendering the Familiar Strange*?"

Jordan started to drift away from me. "Actually, it's cool to be with somebody who isn't maxed out on this stuff. All I have to do is look at it through your eyes."

"And you know what you'll see if you do that? A bed."

As she circled the piece, sort of wrapping herself in it, I

leaned on the wall. Other people filed by—people dressed in cellophane, people with mustard-colored hair, people wearing what looked like shoe boxes instead of shoes. I wanted to sit down, but I was afraid the only chair in the room was called *Chair*.

Just then Jordan, like a boomerang, came back to me.

"You know," I said, "I suppose you think I'm the one who looks weird around here." I glanced down at my slacks and shiny black loafers. "But if we just stop by the gift shop and get me some gills, I'd be the perfect fish out of water."

"You're fine. Follow me."

She pointed us toward a warehouse-size building about a hundred yards away. We charged up the loading ramp, which led to huge green doors; thump, whomp, thump went the bass. It sounded like a giant was beating a rug. I thought of a word we'd just learned in English class—*pandemonium*. I stopped right in the door.

"C'mon," Jordan said like she was leading a horse. "It's okay."

Just inside, Blue and Hector spotted us.

"Cool!" they said in unison.

Jordan looked flustered. "It's just a costume. For tonight. Big deal."

She pointed. "Have you guys been around yet? We're just starting. Want to come?" She fell into Hector's lap and applied the back of one hand to her forehead. "Sumbuddy push me," she drawled.

Blue pointed to one handle of the wheelchair and I took the other.

"Hey, Jordan," said a man with a stuffed hen strapped to his head.

"Hi, Maurice. Cool hat."

"Part of my Barnyard Series."

I watched him wander away. "How did he get here?"

Blue looked at me. "Huh?"

"Did he carry that thing in a bag and then put it on, or did he wear it? If he wore it, tell me he didn't come on the bus."

Blue shrugged. "What's the difference? He's an artist."

"He's a grown man with a chicken on his head. He needs supervision."

We plunged ahead. Right in front of us stood a flat, rickety-looking table. Concrete mushrooms were scattered all over it.

"Get it?" Jordan asked.

Hector guessed. "Stoned?"

"That's stupid." She let her head fall back and talked up to me like she was doing the backstroke. "You into drugs at all?" she asked. "Ganja, acid, crack . . ."

I shook my head. "Are you kidding?"

"Good."

The four of us angled toward a Hispanic guy in his thirties wearing big, inky Ray Bans. He stood beside the hood of a Pontiac Firebird decorated with a life-size St. Christopher.

He saluted Jordan. "How you been, babe?"

"All right, Enrique. You?"

"Not bad, not bad. I got a grant—kind of combination General Motors and NEA thing. How about you? I couldn't find your piece. I didn't know you were wearing it."

Jordan started looking at her hands like she'd just found them at the ends of her arms. "Actually I, uh, you know—didn't quite get done."

Everywhere we turned somebody said hi to Jordan or Hector or Blue. They held out one hand for an old-fashioned give-me-some-skin hello, asked about a show, what had happened to a gallery, or when the last day was for a grant application.

Hector pointed. "Let's go see Blue's piece."

"It's okay," Blue said, "but what's really cool is seeing my whole family together. I should have entered them. Called 'em *Walking Crayolas* or something. Some guy with a camera asked my mother if she was the artist." He scratched his beard. "Which in a way I guess she is."

On the way I looked for Mom. As long as I didn't see paramedics, I guessed she was okay.

Blue had done a pencil sketch of a rumpled bed. Every fold and wrinkle and shadow. It made most of the other stuff look like it'd been created by chimps in boxing gloves.

I turned to him. "Wow!"

Blue grinned. "Thanks."

"It's really good," said Jordan. Then she looked down at her boots. Then she wrapped both arms around herself like she was cold. The red and green lights colored her pale skin as she turned away.

Hector looked at Blue who looked at Hector.

"What?" I asked.

They shook their heads. "Nothing. It's nothing."

Jordan took a deep breath. "Dad says Blue is just about the best pure draftsman he's ever seen."

I felt her breath on my cheek. "What does he say about you?"

"He says I'm not disciplined."

"Is he kidding? Don't you work all the time?"

She looked up at me. "I don't finish, though. That's the kind of discipline he means. The kind where you finish."

Just then Blue's dad ambled up. In his sandals and overalls he looked like the last of the Dead-heads. He gave Jordan a hug, nodded at me, then asked Hector, "What's the Frost Ogre up to now?"

Hector fished in the soft book bag slung over the left side of his red chair and handed him a sketchbook. Blue's father opened it and held it so Jordan and I could see, too.

The pages were filled with sketches and dialogue, so much dialogue that the balloons that held it snuggled right up to the people who had sharp, wintery-looking faces. I couldn't read everything, but I did see a couple of cool lines like "New Euphemisms!" and "Try to punch the bags under your eyes if you're so tough."

"Far out," said Blue's father, reading fast until he got to a blank page.

"Will you all excuse me?" Jordan said.

"You okay?" Hector sounded worried.

As she disappeared, Blue asked, "She okay?"

"I'm not sure." Hector put his sketchbook away.

"What's going on?" I asked.

Hector sighed. "The hardware is killing her."

"The what?"

"Hardware. The prizes, the medals. Jordan doesn't have the hardware, so she gets upset sometimes."

"Nobody won any medals tonight."

"People liked my drawing," Blue explained. "My dad dug Hector's strip. She hasn't got anything anybody can like. It gets to her."

"I can't see Jordan crying in the girls' room."

"She doesn't cry. She goes in the hospital."

"You're kidding."

"Not just because of tonight. It's because she works and works and gets zip. It won't come together for her. Or it breaks."

86

Or she's late, I thought. Then I asked, "But weren't there other shows?"

"For Barbie?" he guessed. "Yeah, but she burned it. Took it outside and burned it."

"Should we tell her dad?" asked Blue.

I said that maybe she just had to go to the bathroom.

"No way. I've seen her worse, but . . ."

"So should we tell him?"

"He should notice." Blue sounded mad all of a sudden. "He shouldn't let it go this far."

"Cool it," said Hector. "Here she comes."

Jordan had washed her face and maybe her hair, because she was wet and shiny from the neck up. She walked right up to us. "I'm okay. It's no problem. I'm fine. Everything's under control. Don't dial any numbers, especially 911." She looked at me. "Did they talk about me?"

"Just about that terrible night and the spacecraft and the brain probe."

Jordan laughed so loud that people turned and stared, and believe me, in that crowd with that noise level getting stared at was kind of an accomplishment.

"Good answer," said Blue, sounding like a game show host.

Jordan hung one arm around my neck like a scarf. "We're going to find my dad. You guys want to come?"

"We'll stay here," said Hector. "Right, Blue?"

"Yeah, right. You guys go on."

"Want to see what the great Drew Archer finished?" She underlined the last word as she pulled me along.

"Are you okay? We could sit down if you want."

"Nah. I'm fine."

My mom and her dad stood about twenty yards away. They were holding blue cups and looking at a big, three-paneled painting: first, a statuelike couple in togas kissed; next, two Swiss kids—the knickknack kind—leaned until their lips met; finally, a white lifeguard knelt on the sand and gave mouth-to-mouth resuscitation to a black woman.

"So he took some pictures and had them enlarged," I said. "Big deal."

"Those are oils," said Jordan.

"You're kidding. He painted that?"

"Not only painted it; he *finished* painting it."

We wandered for a little bit. Jordan nodded at people. Finally I said, "Look, this is probably a stupid question, because I don't know anything about anything much less art, but why isn't your stop-and-go bra an art piece? I mean, you're kind of exhibiting it, aren't you? Like your dad and Blue?"

"Not really. It's just for tonight."

We rounded a corner, stopped in front of an inflatable elephant wrapped in cellophane: *Dumbo to Go.*

"Why," I blurted, "don't you just make more goofy bras."

She grinned a kind of wicked half-grin. "I beg your pardon?"

"Okay, not goofy. Artistic. Satiric. I don't know. Just create more bras. Wouldn't a lot of them make for one piece? Like one stone mushroom is stupid; a hundred stone mushrooms is . . ."

"Well, it's not the same."

"Really? Why not?"

"Well, they don't show well. I mean, what would I do—hang 'em on the wall? Keep running back behind a scrim and changing?"

I pointed over my shoulder. "Do like that guy did with that sex and violence movie-in-the-belly-button thing. Get a bunch of mannequins. It'd look cool. I mean, why not? From what I've seen, anything goes down here, right?"

Jordan frowned as her father spotted us and waved. We started that way as a woman wearing her old prom dress over a Dr. Goodbody neck-to-toe anatomy body stocking started talking to him.

Half her illustrated lungs showed above the ruffled top. Jordan's dad was shaking his head as we cruised up.

"No, thanks," he said firmly.

She brandished a clipboard with AAC printed at the top. "But you're the caliber of artist we need. If people like you aren't against censorship, who is? And if you're not against it, what kind of artist are you?" Her face was as red as her ulnar artery.

"I'm the kind of artist who gets the work done," Drew said evenly. "I have only so much energy, and I use it that way."

Then he walked over to a nearby piece titled *Saturday Night in Medusaville*, stuck his tongue out, and inspected it in the mirror. Frowning, he reached into a front pocket, took out a pillbox, and swallowed something.

The clipboard floated our way. "Old enough to vote, I hope?"

I shook my head. "I sure would if I could," said Jordan. "See me in two years."

All of a sudden the music got louder.

Jordan tugged at my arm. "Want to dance?"

"Last time we danced, I fell down."

"I'll lead this time."

The music gushed out of the speakers and into our pores. We swayed to a long cut. Jordan grinned at me; I grinned back.

"Cool music," she said.

"UB40."

"Really? That's the name of the song?"

"The group."

"You can actually tell one reggae group from another?"

"Sometimes."

She poked me with one finger, but just kidding around. "You're not supposed to have a better ear than me, buddy."

I found myself doing a fancy little step and ended up right beside her.

"So this," she shouted, "is how they really dance up north. I thought you didn't go out."

"Just to this one club." I didn't tell her it was called Tony's Bedroom: no cover, no minimum, no band, no crowd.

Jordan wiped her forehead. "Wanna get some fresh air? I'm about poached."

I followed her until the dancers thinned out. We stepped through a huge door. The loading dock was quiet but packed. I heard the scratchy whir of a lighter. I heard the squeak of leather jackets. We looked toward the industrial section of town where huge trucks bent around corners.

"Is this really the dark," I whispered, "or did somebody paint it?"

"Maybe I ought to turn this thing off." Jordan reached, and her bra went dark.

At last!

I looked down at the old iron bars that made a railing, then touched it with one finger.

"It's okay," she said. "It's not a site-specific installation."

"So this isn't called *Rendering the Familiar Rusty*."

"No."

"Therefore I can lean on it."

"Yes."

I heard her sigh; I felt her shudder.

"Are you okay?" I asked. "I mean before in there, you looked a little . . ."

"I'm all right now. I was just sorry that I didn't have anything ready for this show, either. That's all."

"But at least you work on stuff. And you'll finish next time."

"Yeah, right."

"God, Jordan, you're only sixteen and you know exactly what you want to do with your whole life. Blue, too. And Hector. I'd give anything to feel like that. Even Maurice gets up in the morning and puts on his chicken. But I haven't got a clue."

A voice out of the darkness said, "Your story has touched my heart, but your hour's up, pal. Make an appointment for next week."

Jordan choked back a laugh. I said, "Sorry."

Just then my mother called, "Tony! Are you out here? Jordan? Drew Archer wants to get home."

Jordan groaned and let her head fall against my chest. "Let's hang out tomorrow," she blurted.

"Really?"

"Sure. It wouldn't be a date or anything, we'd just . . ."

"Right, we'd just hang out."

"Maybe brainstorm a little."

"Brainstorm? About what?"

"About some more bras. Different kinds. I liked what you said in there. One bra's a costume, ten are an art piece."

"Did I say that?"

"Maybe you're like my muse."

"I thought muses were girls."

"Tony?"

"We're out here, Mom! We're coming."

"I'll just stop by," Jordan said, "sometime after noon. I've got to work in the morning."

〰〰〰〰

Drew Archer drove home slowly. He and Mom talked a little. Jordan slept through it all, nodding off the minute we got into the car. On the freeway, I watched the bars of light move across her face.

Twenty minutes later, we pulled up in front of our house. Drew turned off the engine, got out, and very politely walked around to the other side of the car.

Jordan rubbed her face. "Where are we?"

"At the ugliest condo in the world."

"Did I drool?" she asked, feeling her chin.

"We all drooled so you wouldn't feel bad."

"I'll see you tomorrow, okay?"

I shook hands with Jordan's father, and said thank you. Mom and I waved as they drove away.

When we got inside, my mother went right to the counter, collapsed onto a stool, and laid her head on her arms.

"My God," she moaned. "This has been the strangest day of my life."

"I'll second that." I put a couple of brownies on a plate, poured two glasses of milk, and set everything between us.

"Are you tired?" she asked. "I'm exhausted." She lifted her head a little. "Did you understand any of that art?"

"Probably not."

"Did you see those rags in the corner?"

"Uh-huh. That was called *The Closer She Got to the Sun, the Hotter Her Breath Became.*"

"They just looked like rags. Dirty rags."

"They were rags."

Mom sat up straighter. "And did you see that boy sitting

in the water? I was afraid he was going to catch his death of cold."

"That was Yusef. Jordan knew him."

"Well, Yusef came up to me dripping wet and said that I was living art. He said my title was *Exceedingly Sling-Backs*." She lifted one foot and let her shoe fall off. "I didn't know whether to be flattered or insulted."

"I'll tell you one thing—that whole bunch is either really nuts or they've got more nerve than I'll ever have." I glanced at Mom, who was massaging her temples. "Drink your milk, okay? It'll help you sleep."

She shook her head. "I'll need a Valium tonight. First, Jordan and her light show, then her father and his hypochondria, then rags with a title."

"Did you get along with Drew Archer?"

She took a long sip of milk. "That's the odd part. We *did* get along. His painting was marvelous, easily the best thing there. And he's very knowledgeable about art without being stuffy." She pushed her hair back and looked for her reflection in the glass. "He's not interested in me at all, I could tell that. But he listened to everything I said, and looked right at me when I talked. For a clearly unbalanced person, he's very good company."

"Yeah, I know what you mean. Jordan and I are going to hang out tomorrow."

Mom pushed her half-empty glass away. "And do what?"

"Hanging out *is* something, Mom."

"Is this a date?"

"No way. Besides not being the date type, she's not even my type."

"Are you going to be alone with her?"

"I don't know. Why?"

"You're fifteen now, almost a man. And Jordan's sixteen

and almost out of her mind." She looked at her hands. "Did Bill ever talk to you about . . . you know."

Oh, *that*. "No, but it's okay. I know plenty from school. And, anyway, with an electric friend, you don't have to worry about birth control, just whether you're grounded or not."

"I shouldn't worry, should I. You're a very responsible boy." She patted me, then sighed. "I've got such a headache."

"Go to bed. I'll clean up down here."

I watched her climb the stairs, heard her bedroom door close. I rinsed the milk glasses and wrapped up the last four brownies. Then I turned out the light.

The kitchen—any kitchen—was my favorite room. I liked looking around it even in the dark. It was something that Drew Archer could have painted: slabs of shadow on the checkered floor, moonlight on the chrome, two knives crossed like oars.

I glanced at the phone. Who else could I tell?

I punched the seven numbers, then sank to the floor again while the message played.

"Hi. I've, uh, talked to you before. Not that you're going to remember or anything. Or care. Which is fine. I'm calling because I just had the weirdest day of my life. First this girl shows up wired like a traffic light, then we go to an unbelievable art show with all kinds of loonballs, who she knows, of course. And I end up dancing with her and dancing pretty well, actually, and then on the way home she's asleep in the car and I can't keep my eyes off her 'cause she looks almost pretty."

I found myself holding on to the receiver like it was the safety bar at Space Mountain, so I took a deep breath.

"I guess all I'm trying to say is that she's the strangest girl I ever met. I mean strange. *Really* strange. But I'm going to see her tomorrow, and this is the unbelievable part—I can't wait!"

━━━━

The next afternoon I was in the living room supposedly doing homework, but thinking about how to get out of the house before the lecture about the dangers of high voltage underwear.

Next door the Reeds were arguing. Their voices leaked through the walls.

"Dad, I don't want to play tennis!" Johnny shouted. "I'm sick of tennis."

Mom came out of the kitchen. She was staring at a tall glass of I-don't-know-what.

"The neighbors are restless."

"Maybe they've been drinking extract of pond slime, too."

"Very funny. This is some of that stuff for my weeping lungs."

"Try it with a bagel."

She shook her head. "I had two last night. Did I wake you?"

I shook my head.

"Well, I couldn't sleep, so I got up, watched "Dr. Quinn, Medicine Woman" on tape, and pigged on bagels. Isn't that pitiful? Forty-two years old, home alone on a Saturday night watching Dr. Mike tear up her underwear for bandages. God, I wish I had the petticoat concession in that town."

Just then the phone rang. Mom picked it up, listened, and asked, "Who shall I say is calling?" Then she held the phone at arm's length. I didn't even get to say hello.

"Tony?" Jordan blurted. "I can't come over, after all."

"What's wrong?"

"Nothing. I just . . . I've been trying to . . ."

"To what? Are you home?"

I heard her take a couple of deep breaths before she said, "I spread myself way too thin. I mean, I just want to do everything, you know? Everything. Like getting caught up with this piece for the October show, then switching gears and wanting to do something nice for Dad before you and I got together. But now it's just all . . . I mean he's going to be home and you should see this place."

I shifted the phone to the other, cooler ear. "What are you trying to do?"

She almost screamed it. "Cook!"

"Is that all?"

"But I can't. I can't do anything now. I get like paralyzed and I shake and . . ."

"What did you want to cook?"

"Huh?"

I repeated it.

"Uh, meat loaf."

"Did you follow the recipe?"

"Well, no, but you can cook, so I thought how hard can it be."

"Thanks a lot."

"Well, you make it sound easy. I thought an hour at the most. Now it's two hours and I'm nowhere and if Dad sees this kitchen he's going to kill me."

"Look, just stay where you are. I'll come over."

"No, it's too late. Everything's ruined. Dad'll be home. And I look terrible."

"What are you wearing, a shirt with paint on it and ugly shoes? Wow. I'm shocked."

I listened to her breathe or, to be more precise, pant. "I take on too many things. I get one idea and that makes me get another one and they all seem good and then I think about the show last night and beat myself up for not having anything ready and—"

"When is your dad coming home?"

"Umm, four, probably. And I just wanted to surprise him."

"Meet me at the store."

"What store?"

"The grocery store—Von's. You know, big building on the corner full of food."

"But there's not enough time!" She said it like she was working feverishly in the lab and aliens were beating on the door with their tentacles.

"Four o'clock, are you kidding? I can cook ten things before four o'clock. Just meet me, okay? Say you will."

Finally she said it and I hung up.

My mother looked at me, one of *those* looks. "What now?"

"Meltdown. She said it'd happen, and I guess it almost did."

"What's it got to do with you?"

"Mom, she needs a favor. I'm only going to help her cook something."

She followed me to the door. "Be careful. Tony, do you hear me? Be careful."

〰〰〰

She wasn't in front of Von's, so I paced for a while, walking all the way to Locust on one side, then Mariposa on the other. Behind me, on the windows of the market, huge red numbers loomed like the idols of Easter Island.

Then I spotted Jordan's green Honda wagon coasting into a parking space. She got out, looked around blearily, then got back in again.

I jogged over, tapping on the back window so she'd know

I was there. I sure didn't want to scare her; I was afraid she'd just lift off like something at the Science Fair.

"I didn't think you were here yet," she said without looking up.

"You're staring at the dashboard."

"I got out."

I reached through the open window and laid one hand on her shoulder.

"I'm so screwed up," she whispered.

Tugging at her, I got her to look up at me. "Are you taking anything?" I asked.

She shook her head. "I told you I don't do drugs. I'm nuts enough."

"Is this the meltdown you were talking about the other day?"

"Uh-huh."

"It's not so bad." I opened the car door. "So c'mon out. Say hello to the world."

She didn't look up. "Can't it come to me?"

I held the door for her. She looked pretty rough—bony, pale, smudged, jumpy.

I pointed. "How many people in that car?"

She shielded her eyes. "What?"

"In that blue Ford Taurus there. How many people?"

"Four?"

"Good." Then I pointed to the big store window. "How much are those apples on sale?"

She scowled. "Sometimes I throw up when I get like this."

"I knew I shouldn't have worn these new shoes."

She bent over, breathed through her nose, went whoosh a couple of times.

I put one hand on her shoulder. "C'mon."

She held her stomach with both hands. "I'm going to join P.T.A."

"You're not a parent."

"Pop-Tarts Anonymous."

I pointed. "Let's go to the store."

"This doesn't freak you out, does it."

"I've seen worse."

"It makes Blue and Hector nuts. Dad just calls his internist who calls the hospital." Her breath shuddered going out. "I don't need any stupid doctor."

I put my arm around her shoulder. "Let's go shopping."

"There's time? Really?"

"Sure."

She leaned into my T-shirt. "You smell good."

"One of us has to. It's the law."

"I'm hopeless. I'm not good for anything."

"And I was hoping for fashion tips for the holidays."

Just inside the big sliding door, I could feel the heat still on my back, the conditioned air on my face. I looked at the huge displays looming at the entrance of every aisle: a thousand Oreos, mountains of Sun Chips, enough 7-Up for every upset stomach in North America.

"What did you want to cook?" I asked.

"Uh, meat loaf, you know, but with turkey. And a . . ." She stalled.

"First word?"

"Green."

"Salad?"

"Right. But I had trouble with the turkey."

"They have ground turkey here?"

She waited a second. "Oh."

I turned to her. "You bought a whole turkey? What do

you think *loaf* means, Jordan? That the meat just lies around and watches TV?"

She shook her head. "I only bought, like, parts."

"How were you going to grind it?"

"I don't know, okay?" She pulled her hand away from mine.

I took it back. "What do you have at home: an onion, celery, bread crumbs, a pepper, a . . . ?"

"I bought celery. I think. But by the time I got home from here this morning and got started, I'd thought of something else I wanted to put in the show that's coming up and after that I kind of collapsed and when I woke up everything I'd bought was lying on the counter and it was all kind of warm and gooshy and . . ."

"We'll just start from scratch."

Back at the meat counter I took a number while Jordan looked around in that way she had.

"No art," I insisted.

"Sorry."

When it was our turn, I asked the butcher to grind me some fresh turkey. "From the back, please. The stuff out here looks a little tired."

He peered over his bifocals. "It's all fresh."

"I'm the cook here, okay?"

Shoulders slumped, he trudged away. Jordan leaned into the cold glass and shuddered. "Dad says it's okay to eat meat as long as you acknowledge the suffering that you're contributing to."

"He must be fun at a barbecue."

The butcher showed me three turkey breasts with the ribs attached. I leaned forward, sniffed, and pointed. "These two."

"Just came in," he admitted.

When he turned away, Jordan said, "That was cool. How'd you know how to do that?"

"Bought some bad chicken once, read a book, asked a couple of butchers. It's no big deal."

"You always say that, but it *is* a big deal. I couldn't do it."

"Aw, you could learn in about ten minutes."

She shook her head vigorously. "I could smell those two pieces of turkey for a week and never know which one was best."

"After a week, everybody'd know."

As we cruised up the soups and sauces aisle, Jordan asked, "You don't mind pushing the cart?"

I stopped to read the labels on a couple of jars of pasta sauce.

"Why should I?"

"A lot of guys mind big-time. Some woman's-work thing."

"Well, this is a very masculine cart: mag wheels, see? C'mon. Just a few more things." I pointed. "Get me an onion, will you? And don't get mad just because they're all alike. Onions are really a deeply subversive vegetable."

"Where are you going?"

I waved the red sauce. "I'm going to trade this in. I'll just be a minute. And make sure the celery's not limp, okay?"

Three aisles over I brooded over sauces for a while, finally deciding that I could sauté my own mushrooms and peppers. Then I strolled back to the produce section, where Jordan had an audience: three or four kids and their folks.

She'd found an almost empty bin and had made an Indian chief: headdress of corn, a quarter of purple cabbage at his forehead, mustard greens for his collar, a walnut eye, bean sprout lips. A small leek here, a loose lettuce leaf there.

She worked fast, her tongue out. The kids watched, mesmerized. Down went a summer squash, part of a carrot, one broccoli crown.

Finally she stepped back. "Arcimboldo did it first," she told them. "Get your folks to take you to the library and look him up. Fabulous stuff." Then she spotted me. "Oh, hi. I, uh, got distracted."

"It's okay. Go ahead. I'll get the other stuff."

She skipped, literally skipped, toward me. "No, no. I'm done. And I'm fine. Got my second, third, and fourth wind all at the same time; you're better than one of Dad's Energy Bars."

~~~~~

Twenty minutes later we pulled up in front of a duplex on Charter Oak. "Guess which side is mine," she urged.

On the left, one calla lily stood in a blue pot. On the right were part of a bicycle, a wrought iron chair, palm fronds fanned like a bridge hand, a couple of hubcaps, three or four cinder blocks, a flattened squirrel, two dead jade plants, an open book.

On her porch, she fumbled with a key, then let the door swing open. I looked over her shoulder.

"Does the Environmental Protection Agency know about this?" I asked.

"Everything out of place and a place for every out-of-it thing."

Two mismatched chairs were pulled up to a long library table. On it sat a couple of answering machines, about a gallon of Elmer's glue, two telephones, cassettes, and about a yard of water-stained velvet. More palm fronds cluttered the floor, some cut in half, some split down the middle. A refrigerator with its door knocked off lurked in one corner beside some headphones.

The carpet was a minefield of old windup clocks, parts of Barbie dolls, pages ripped from *Interview* and *Soldier of Fortune*, vases on their sides, blocks of paraffin, the bell of a clarinet, silverware bent at right angles, half a mannequin growing out of a papier-mâché tree trunk, a small reel-to-reel tape machine spilling tape onto prints by some French guy and between two bowling pins. Inside a medicine cabinet she'd stacked seven or eight baby shoes, then a little stuffed penguin, plastic colored Easter eggs nesting in a huge toupee, a prosthetic shin. On the wall she'd tacked a computer-generated banner that said HUGO TO MY HEAD.

She was already nodding, agreeing with herself, as she decided, "We're cooking next door; I gotta clean up over there, anyway."

Drew's place was left brain to her right: polished hardwood floors, one mostly lavender carpet under an oak table with legs as elegant as a doe's. On the walls hung his paintings: a grass green John Deere tractor, the corner of a spotless kitchen, the fender of a Honda Accord reflecting a mechanic's frown. All done with as much detail as any photograph.

I headed toward the kitchen, which was a low-grade disaster.

"What's all the flour for?" I asked.

"I was going to cook. I thought you always needed flour when you cook."

"On the floor?"

"I dropped it."

"No kidding." I stacked pots, one inside the other, and carried them to the sink. "And why so many of these?"

"On television, they've always got a lot of pots."

"Your dad has nice stuff," I said, rinsing off a Circulon skillet.

"Does it really matter?" she asked, tumbling the vegetables onto a white cutting board.

I handed her things to dry. "Cheap pans don't always heat evenly."

"Yeah, Dad won't use cheap brushes when he paints, either."

As I swept up the floor and sponged off cabinets, I watched her inspect a stalk of celery, turning it over slowly, looking at it from every angle. Finally I asked, "What?"

"Remember that piece at the Ironworks show, the one that wanted to render the familiar strange? Same thing, sort of."

I handed her a knife. "How about rendering the familiar small."

We worked side-by-side for a while without saying anything. The kitchen began to smell good, with steam rising off the sautéed onions. Every now and then she'd lean into me or I'd lean into her. She broke eggs into a yellow bowl as I added sauce and turkey and started to knead everything together.

"So this is what you like about it!" she said without pausing.

I knew what she meant—the great smell of the kitchen, how the window steamed up just a little, the slippery pepper and its deep green, translucent onions, heft of the skillet and saucepan, glint of the knife blade: the doing and the not thinking.

"When's your dad coming home?"

She glanced at the clock. "Pretty soon, probably."

"Then we'll do individual loaves and just pop 'em in the microwave. They won't be nice and crusty, but they'll be okay."

A few minutes later we stood in front of the double-sided

sink. She washed the long leaves of romaine and I rubbed fresh garlic around and around a battered wooden bowl.

"Tony, remember how you handled me at the market, that how-many-people-in-the-car stuff?"

"Uh-huh."

"Where did you learn to do that? I swear to God I was about one microstress level away from a week at Huntington Memorial."

"I learned from Mom."

"She taught you?"

I shook my head. "I taught myself. Mom could get like she wasn't here anymore, you know? Just out in space or something. Gone. That's how you were."

"Tell me about it. Anyway, you were great. Thanks."

"You're welcome."

She looked right at me. I looked right back. She smiled. I smiled.

"Do you feel comfortable with me?" she asked.

"Yeah. I have no idea why, but yeah."

"Really comfortable? Like we've been friends for a long time. *Good* friends."

I dried one of Drew Archer's expensive knives. "Yeah."

"I think I want to kiss you."

I looked over at her. She was staring down at the soapy water. "But not," she said, "like those kids at school who lean on the wall and lick each other."

That made me laugh.

"Well, you know what I mean, Tony."

"I wanted to kiss you last night when we were out on that loading dock."

"But not now?"

"Sure, now, too."

She turned so we were facing each other. But she didn't look up at me. Instead, she stared at my T-shirt.

"What?" I asked.

"I don't know. I just . . . I don't know. I want to. I'm just not sure this is in my ed plan."

I reached for her hand. "Why don't we just wait."

"Really?"

"This friendship thing feels pretty good. I mean, to me, anyway."

"Me, too. It feels great. I mean I'm friends with Hector and Blue, but . . ."

I finished for her. "Not like this?"

"Yeah."

Just then the timer on the microwave went off. I rescued one of the little loaves with a spatula.

"We'd better try some," I said. "If it's not any good, we'll call Domino's."

We ate at the same kind of counter that Mom and I had in our condo, but the tile on this one wasn't perfect on purpose; it was cut in half and busted up and mismatched so that when I glanced down there was always something to look at or to feel.

I watched her take a bite.

"It's great," she said.

I tried some. It *was* good. I wolfed down some more. Then I looked over at her. "You don't think I'm a wuss, do you? I mean deep down you didn't want me to just grab you and kiss you. Right?"

Jordan hopped off the chrome stool. "Did you want that?"

If I'd had a phone in my hand, if I'd been talking to Confess-O-Rama, I would've said, "Jordan, I want everything—I want to be friends, I want to kiss you, I want to stay in West Paradise, I want to know what to do with my life."

106

Instead I murmured, "I asked you first."

She reached for my hand, almost tipping over my glass. We both grabbed, and milk sloshed out. She ran for a sponge; I made a little dam with my fingers. I think we were both glad there was something to do.

When things were cleaned up, I tapped on the uneven counter with my butter knife. "Did your dad do this?"

"When we moved here a couple of years ago and we were pretty sure it was going to be for good, we had a kind of party. Different people came and brought pieces of things." She pointed out the handle for a teacup, then a piece of a mug with a cat's face, then a chunk as blue as Chicken Little's sky.

"From Angie," she said, pointing, "Victor, Enrique, Amy, Amy's kid. Dad says that every time your plate rocks a little or your Pepsi won't sit straight, you can think about somebody who loves you."

I looked down at my plate decorated around the edges with *X*'s and *O*'s.

"When we went downtown to that art show," I said, "you knew everybody and everybody knew you." I tapped the surface of the counter again. "And every now and then it hits me how *I* couldn't have a party; *I* couldn't ask old friends to bring pieces of stuff, because I don't have any old friends."

She touched my forearm. "You don't write to anybody from the school before this one or call or . . ."

I shook my head firmly. "Nope."

"Was your mom really so bad off that you couldn't . . ."

I pushed my plate away. "If I didn't cook, she didn't eat. If I didn't check, she'd get her meds mixed up. So I'm telling kids I can't go here or I can't do that because I have to be home. Then when she did get better, well, by then it was too late; everybody was used to counting me out."

Jordan tugged at me until we were face-to-face. "Look, here's what we'll do: I'll call up a bunch of people and have 'em come over; you'll meet 'em, and then they'll be your friends, too."

"You can't have a party for no reason, Jordan."

"Are you kidding? Sure, you can."

"They'd know it was for me. I'd be embarrassed."

"They're not going to know it's for you. First of all, it's not for you; Dad and I haven't had a party in a long time. Second of all, you'll be with me."

I shook my head. "That's not how you make friends. You don't just go to a party and collect 'em."

"Are you kidding? Half the friends in the world met at parties. My dad met my mom at a party."

"But what do I do besides be with you?"

"That's pitiful. You have a good time. You dance. You eat. You make fun of people's outfits. You tell jokes. You lie."

"I could cook something."

"Fine."

We each pushed some meat loaf around on our plates. Then I asked, "You'd really give a party just for me, just so I could meet people?"

"Yes."

I took a couple of quick bites. Man, the last time anybody gave a party just for me, there'd been a pony and a clown!

"But I'm only going to invite guys and really ugly girls. Because I don't want you to like anybody else. Isn't that wonderfully politically incorrect?"

"I don't want to like anybody else."

"So I can go ahead and ask Cindy Crawford?"

I perked up. "*The* Cindy Crawford?"

Jordan reached for a stalk of celery and slapped me on the

108

arm with it. I was defending myself with a carrot stick when we heard a car pull into the driveway and the solid thunk of a slammed door.

"At last," she said.

I started tugging at my shirt, smoothing the front. "Why am I nervous? We didn't do anything."

She held out one hand, making it quiver like Marlo the Mesmerizer. In her deepest voice she said, "Fathers can see into the hearts of teenage boys and read their secret thoughts."

"Oh, great."

Then the front door swung open. "How'd it go, Dad?" she asked.

Her father looked a little haggard. "Okay, I guess. We'll see when the paint dries. What have you two been up to?"

"Cooking," she blurted.

"Nothing," I blurted.

"Cooking nothing, huh. That couldn't have taken long."

Drew lifted something muddy-looking out of the refrigerator and took a bite.

"What smells good?"

"Not me," said Jordan automatically. "So it must be the meat loaf. Tony made it. I helped, though. I intimidated the celery. Anyway, it's all for you, 'cause you've been working hard."

He kissed his daughter on the cheek, put one hand on my shoulder. "That's marvelous."

"Listen, I better go. Mom'll wonder what happened."

Drew was cutting himself a slice of meat loaf. "Bye, Tony," he said absently. "Thanks for dinner."

Jordan opened the front door, let me through, closed it behind us. It was almost dark. The cool, damp air felt a little frayed as she put her arms around my neck.

"I should have called her," I said.

"Does she still worry?"

"Are you kidding? It's like her job."

Jordan sagged. "Oh, God. That reminds me of my job." She looked toward her side of the duplex and pretended to pass out.

I propped her against the door. "Are you going to finish this one?"

She grinned. "What a rude friend. Yes, finishing is definitely part of the plan."

I turned her around and pointed her toward the other door. "So maybe you should go to work."

"It was your idea," Jordan said over the noise of forty people scooping dip with flimsy chips and Billy Joel claiming that he didn't start the fire.

I looked down at her new bra featuring big sealed-beam headlights in a kind of seaworthy rigging. "My idea?"

"Yeah, after what you said at Dada last month about me making more of these. So I thought of this when we were cooking for my dad last week."

"I said put 'em on a mannequin."

110

"I'm trying them out."

"Are you tall?" Hector asked when he rolled up beside me. "Or am I in a wheelchair?"

I grinned and we shook hands. His gloves—the ones with the fingers cut off—matched his red shirt.

"What do you think of this bra?" I pointed.

"Cool."

"Really?"

"Absolutely," he said. "It destroys metaphor. Now guys can't say, 'Look at the headlights on that one' without being literal."

Jordan smirked as I admitted, "I'm never going to understand the art world. I'm hopeless."

"You're nice." She consoled me.

"That'll look good on my tombstone: Hopeless but Nice."

Hector pointed to a tall girl with catsup-colored hair. "Jordan, is that the one from P.H.S.? The one you said wanted to be the paralegal?"

"Uh-huh."

"I'm going to roll over there and put some moves on her. We're meant for each other. She's paralegal; I'm paraplegic."

"Good luck with a line like that."

We watched Rochelle trudge around wedging chastity fliers between the slow dancers. Then a guy in an Act-Up T-shirt wandered over with some of my potato salad on a little red plate.

Jordan introduced us. "Jack, Tony. Tony, Jack."

"This is fabulous, Tony. Drew Archer said you might share the recipe."

I shrugged. "Well, almost any recipe'll do if you add a little fresh dill. Just don't use Idaho potatoes. Try the little red ones. And don't boil them too long."

"What about this meat loaf?" asked a woman who had a

little gold ballpoint poised. "Drew Archer said that you said there was a secret?"

"Oh, yeah. Applesauce."

"No!" She said it like I'd admitted that I played team tennis with the pope.

"Yes. Like half a cup. Just make sure it's only applesauce, no sugar or anything like that."

As she wrote furiously on a blue napkin, Jordan whispered, "Are you having a good time?"

"Yes," I admitted.

"Everybody likes you."

"Everybody likes *you*," I said. "And I'm with you."

"So? That's how you start making friends."

"Yeah, but . . ." Just then I saw Mom in what she called her little blue dress. She was talking to Sheila, Barry's mother, in her standard black outfit.

I knew if Mom saw Jordan's headlights, she'd probably never let me use our car. I could just hear her saying, "Why not just wait until your girlfriend gets a steering wheel and an engine. Then you can just drive *her* around."

I pulled Jordan toward the kitchen.

"What?" she demanded.

"I just, uh, want to get a good look at this new creation of yours. The light's better in here."

She tugged her arm free. "Get serious. Art still freaks you out, doesn't it."

I saw my mom lean toward Sheila Larson and laugh. "Well, maybe. But then I need to look closer."

She made a face. "I was on my way to the bathroom, if you don't mind."

"Great!"

"You haven't been into the cooking sherry, have you, Tony?"

"Just go. Take your time. See you later."

Mom and Sheila slipped between dancers and went out the front door together. I sagged against the counter.

Drew Archer appeared, handed me an orange slice, and showed me the one he'd crammed into his mouth to make a big orange grin.

"Am I going to have to have you eighty-sixed from the juice bar?" I asked.

He smiled at me. He draped one arm across my shoulders, something Bill used to do after we'd played ball together. I couldn't breathe for a second.

"She's going to see her eventually," he said.

I just stood there with his arm around me. Finally I stammered, "Mom is, you mean. Going to see Jordan."

He nodded. "Isn't that what we're talking about?"

"You don't miss much, do you? I'm just afraid that Jordan's going to upset her, that's all."

He reached for a blue corn chip. I watched his arm float away. "Some good art," he said, "is supposed to provoke. And Jordan's provocative by nature. When she was a little girl, she used to stab her dolls and leave them lying on the walk with catsup leaking out of their wounds. She'd wait all day by the window for the mailman, just to see the look on his face."

"So you don't worry about her."

He shook his head.

"I wonder why I do?"

"You're used to worrying. You choose to be involved with the Universe's plan for your mother."

"The universe."

"With a capital *U*."

"Its plan for her?"

113

"One dead husband after another. You choose to get involved in that drama and to become who you are."

"Mr. Archer, wouldn't anybody worry if his mother's husbands kept dropping like flies?"

He chewed the last of his orange and threw the rind away. "Not necessarily."

"Let me get this straight: Mr. Universe with a capital U has a plan for my mother, and part of that plan is that she's supposed to be sad almost all the time?"

"Emerson said that tragedy consists of temperament, not events."

"What's that supposed to mean."

"That it's not what happens, it's how you handle what happens."

"Mom did the best she could!"

"No one said that she didn't."

I looked down at my shoes. "Sorry."

"Don't be. You're defending your mother; most people would."

"Meaning not everybody. Like who wouldn't?"

"Oh, people perhaps who chose to ride the waves of imagined conflict like the halcyon bird."

"A bird, huh."

Drew Archer smiled at me. "You're a remarkable young man."

"You're not going to hug me, are you?"

He laughed and reached for a piece of raw cauliflower. "No."

It was my turn to grab a celery stick. I listened to music— a Cranberries CD—and looked at the crowded room. I saw Hector talking to the red-haired girl and laughing. Jordan was dancing with a tall guy in gold pants. Blue came in, caught my eye, and waved.

I looked over at Jordan's dad. "This is a cool party."

He sounded very solemn. "The Universe means for it to be cool." Then he laughed, sounding really tickled with himself.

"You're weird, Mr. Archer. But I like talking to you."

"You need another man in your life. And right now. Fifteen's an important age for that."

Boy, he could kid around one second, then nail you with something the next.

"Gee, I don't know about . . ."

"I'm too selfish," he said. "And too weird for you right now. So look for it from an unlikely source."

"It?"

"Parenting. Advice. A man who takes a real heart-interest in you."

"Drew Archer, excuse me." A woman loomed beside us. Her green sweater looked heavy as turf. "But is this the young man who made the marvelous meat loaf?"

He nodded. "Tony Candelaria, Betty Rich."

She took my hand gingerly, like I was a violinist. "I won't keep you," she said, "but I just wanted to ask if you'd be interested in working with the chef from Casa Pasadena."

"Working? Doing what?"

"In a month or so my husband and I are having a little affair catered by Isabelle Feingarten. Do you know her?"

"No, ma'am."

"She's wonderful. Studied in France, worked in New York. When someone told me you'd made that challenging potato salad, I thought I'd just ask. You'd probably just be doing prep work for her, but . . ."

"No, that'd be cool. I mean, sure. I'd like to. Thanks."

"Well, you two go on with your conversation. I'll call Drew Archer next week and he can give me your number."

When she was gone, I looked at Drew Archer. "Wow, working with a real chef! Did you put her up to that?"

He shook his head. "It's synchronicity."

"Huh?"

"It means that things come along when you need them. People, too."

"Oh, yeah? Why didn't somebody come along three dead stepfathers ago?"

"Somebody probably did; you were just too busy to take their hand."

"So the Universe sent Mrs. Rich over to see if I wanted to chop onions?"

He nodded solemnly. "When it comes to food, you're entirely self-taught, aren't you."

"Not exactly."

"Really? Who showed you the way? Not your mother, she was grieving. Not your stepfathers, because I asked Kathryn. You did it mostly on your own. It's extraordinary, Tony. What an accomplishment."

"Really? You think so?"

"Absolutely."

We grinned at each other for a while. Then he asked, "Am I babbling? Have I had too much no-nitrates wine crushed by the feet of celibate monks?"

"No. Keep talking. I like it."

"Well, then, let's talk about your art—food. Which do you like best: buying it, handling it, or cooking it?"

I thought about that. "All of 'em, I guess. They're different. Maybe working with it, you know? Before it's cooked."

He nodded. "People think I love pictures, but I love paint, too. I like it in its tubes. I like it on the palette. I like it before it has to do anything." He leaned toward a piece of his called *Summer Fun*. A pair of calloused feet hung over the

116

cracked edge of a swimming pool slightly polluted by tanning lotion and sunblock.

As he inspected his own work, I asked, "Did you always know you wanted to be a painter?"

He leaned even closer. "Uh-huh. I tried to do things that made other people happy, but it just didn't work out. So I sold real estate, *and* I painted. I was a waiter, *and* I painted. Then I got lucky. A couple of little shows got good reviews and I saw that if we were careful about how we spent, I could paint full-time."

"Drew Archer?" Someone waved from across the room. "Good-bye. Good-bye, Tony."

He patted me on the shoulder. "You're a big hit tonight."

Once the front door was opened, it turned out to be like one of those doors on a spaceship: it sucked out two girls with identical cornrow hairdos, then a guy in vinyl pants, then the bald man who'd eaten all the pine nuts.

Mr. Wong made his way toward me. "Good-bye, Tony," he said with an almost imperceptible bow. "Come to store sometime, please. Not buy things. Just say hello."

"Sure, thanks. Listen, have you seen my mother?"

"Earlier only."

Gliding away from me, Jordan intercepted him. He took her hand, too, said something, and they both looked my way and smiled. I picked up a clean fork and sampled somebody else's pasta salad.

"Too much oil," I said as Jordan stepped up behind me and slid both arms around my waist.

"On me?"

"On this macaroni. But with that bra, it feels like I just got hit by a Buick."

"Are you having a good time? Are you happy?"

I can't tell you how happy I really am. "Sure."

Just then the front door opened, and with a cackle, Barry lurched through.

"Jordan!" he bellowed, weaving our way.

"Who let him in?"

She shrugged. "I invited his dad because he had my dad on his show about nine times this year, so . . ."

Barry stumbled into us. "You look great tonight. Dance with me, Jordie," he begged.

"Maybe later." She let his big, damp hands rest on the shoulders of her new, blue turtleneck. "But hold it down, okay? If Drew Archer hears you, he'll kick your butt out of here. You're not exactly twenty-one."

He reached for his back pocket, pulled out a T-shirt, and held it up. There was his father's big face above the words Keep Larry in Paradise. "I'll give you one of these if you'll dance with me."

"You're too kind, but no."

"Yeah, wouldn't want to cover up those headlights of yours."

"I don't suppose," said Jordan, "that you see the point."

He lifted both hands like the Creeper and pretended to lunge for her. "I see both points."

"Shut up, Barry," I told him.

Barry started chopping up the air with what he hoped were kung-fu moves. "Oh, yeah? Are you going to make me?"

Blue glided up to him. "C'mon. I gotta go home. I'll drop you on the way."

Barry pulled free. "Don't wanna go home. Wanna dance and make romance."

"Van Morrison," I muttered. " 'Wild Night.' "

Barry tried to snap his fingers. "Good for you," he blurted. Then he glared at me. "Why's Jordan with you and not me, huh? Why?"

I guess he forgot we were going to fight. "I'm taller."

"Only a lil bit."

"I was kidding."

"Let's find your dad," urged Blue.

He wagged his big head. "No. Wanna stay with Jordan. Love Jordan."

Jordan batted his hands away. "Go home, Barry. And don't come around here anymore when you're drunk. I mean it."

"Fine." He straightened up righteously. "Go outside. People outside like me."

We watched him careen toward the open door. Blue started after him, then gave up and turned to me. "Tony? How about the movies Friday night?"

Jordan pointed to herself. "What am I, chopped liver?"

"No, you're an artist who needs to get slides and a proposal to the committee by—"

"I know, Blue, okay?" Jordan snapped. "I know when they need slides." She started to mutter, "Man, I've gotta get a tent, I've gotta get mirrors, I've gotta start editing." She grabbed me. "I'm going next door to work. I'll see you, okay?"

She was gone, so I said to the air, "Okay, I'll just try and find my mom."

Then she was back again. She put her arms around me so tight I couldn't breathe for a second. It was hard to know which would break first—my ribs or the glass in her headlights.

"What's up?"

She just kissed me hard and fast, more like a punch than a kiss, and this time went and stayed gone.

I fell in step with Blue, who was headed for the door, too. "Didn't you just get here?" I asked. "Why are you going home?"

He held up his beeper. "Somebody's sick. Mom and Dad are at a concert. I will be so glad to get out of high school and away from here."

"I'd just like to stay."

"Why can't you?"

"You don't know any Mafiosa, do you? I think I'd like to have somebody break my mother's legs. Then she couldn't leave."

"Yeah, when my folks drop six kids on me and go off like this, it makes *me* want to know some Mafiosa."

We laughed, shook hands, then stepped off the porch and headed in different directions. Out by the street, three grown-ups stood by Larry's sagging Dodge: his once-upon-a-time wife, my mom, and the man himself.

"When we were married," Sheila said to her former husband, "you did too call me every day. And usually when you were on the air."

Mom laughed and shook her head as I cruised up.

"You know everyone?" my mother said, pointing. "Larry, Sheila . . ."

I nodded my way around the semicircle, finishing with my mother, who'd slipped one of Larry's T-shirts over her blue dress.

"Once," Sheila said, "I'm in the tub trying to relax and he calls. He's doing Can You Wear a Miniskirt and Still Serve God, right?" She thumbed her black cowboy hat farther back on her head. "How do I know anything about that?"

"I had to call somebody. My board was dead. Not one red light."

"So you told them I was naked in the bathtub."

"Then they called."

"To talk about my body, Larry. You told them about my body!"

"I said it was beautiful."

"That isn't the point. The point is you told them."

"Well, I'm on talk radio. If nobody calls in to talk, I'm out the door."

Sheila looked at my mother, who was laughing again. "He tells everybody everything. He can't shut up."

"I'd be a much better husband now," Larry assured all of us. "For one thing, I know a lot more about marriage."

"Oh, sure," said his former wife. "Because you did a show on it?"

"A week. I did a whole week. And listen to this—want to know the longest marriage on record? Eighty-six years; of course, they were married when they were five. How about the longest engagement. Couple from Mexico, sixty-seven years. And the wedding that cost the most? Some sheik: he had twenty thousand guests and it lasted a week." He held up his hands like he'd named all the tunes and won a trip to Hawaii. "See?"

"Makes me want to marry you again," said Sheila, pretending to gag herself with an index finger.

I turned to my mother. "I was just thinking of going home. I've got school tomorrow. So I thought I'd find you and, you know, just go. You ready?"

"Almost." She looked right at Larry Deluxe. "You worry me," she said. "Remember, don't ever take the first offer. My third husband handled all his own book contracts, and he never ever took the first thing they put on the table."

"But I'm glad to get any offer. They were thinking about letting me go."

She shook her head. "You don't know that. They let you find it out. It's part of the game. Haven't you read *Getting What You Deserve*?"

"I think so," he said, scratching his head. "Or was that *Getting into the Reserves?*"

"I've got the book at home someplace," Mom said.

"Good, let's go get it."

"Now?"

"No time like the present."

Mom rubbed the bridge of her nose. "Well, I don't know if tonight is . . ."

"Look," said Larry, glancing at me. "You drive, I'll take your mom, and we'll follow you."

"Well, uh, I don't, you know, have a license. I'm just fifteen."

Larry lifted a beer out of a blue ice chest balanced on the trunk of his car and took a long swallow. "You've got a learner's permit, don't you? So I'll ride with you; we'll get acquainted. Your mom can drive my car."

I squirmed.

"He has his permit," said Mom. "But no behind-the-wheel time yet. Anyway, Tony's not that interested in driving."

I just stared at her.

Larry lowered his rose-colored aviator glasses and peered at me.

"Is that true. You're not interested? Somebody see if he's got a pulse. Man, I did a show about milestones, okay? And for every guy who said it was his first sexual experience, two said it was getting their driver's license."

"The address is one thousand Diamond," Mom said. "Meet me there."

Larry took a last sip of Coors, grinned. "I'll just say good-night to the host."

Mom and I started toward our car.

"I'm really too tired to do this tonight," she admitted, putting one hand over her heart. "But on his own, he makes all the wrong moves. When he went to get drinks, Sheila told me he did a Fourth of July show one year."

"So?"

"A fourth of July *fireworks* show."

"Fireworks on the radio. That was his idea?"

"I'm afraid so. He has these . . . gaps, I guess. He's like those sets of encyclopedias you buy at a yard sale: lots of information, but there's always something missing."

Then it hit me—a solution to my problem. A plan. Was this synchronicity, too? "Well, when we get home," I said casually, "I'll make coffee."

"I don't want coffee. I want to find him that book and get him out of there."

"If you're going to stay up late talking about . . . whatever it is you're going to be talking about . . ."

"His contract for KGAB is up for renewal."

"Exactly, then you'll need some coffee. You know, with the cinnamon stick and the whipped cream you like."

Mom stopped and tilted my head toward the streetlight. "Let me see your eyes."

I twisted away. "I never do drugs."

"Then what are you so squirmy about all of a sudden? You act like you've got ants in your pants."

"Ants in my pants? One minute you want to know if I've been smoking ganja; the next it's ants in my pants. Make up your mind, Mom. Am I fifteen or five."

She frowned at me as she fished for her keys. "Ganja. What's 'ganja'?"

"Dope. Grass. Reefer. Chronic."

"Where did you learn all those words. From Jordan?"

"No, in the gym at Daly City High."

"I didn't know you knew words like that."

"There's a lot about me you don't know."

"Tony, what's gotten into you?"

"Nothing. You said you and Larry were going to talk, right? I said I'd make some coffee."

"I meant your attitude. But no one's going to talk. I'm going to lend him a book."

"You loaned Russ a book, remember? The next thing I knew we were in Tucson."

"I am not the United Way. I'm through helping men succeed. I want to succeed myself, for a change." She pointed her car key at me. "So no coffee. I don't know what you're up to, but I don't like it."

◆◆◆◆◆

When Mom went downstairs to look for that book Larry wanted, I started the teakettle, then dove for the phone.

"Confess-O-Rama? I have to make this fast, but you should have been there tonight: everybody's shaking my hand and fighting over my potato salad and offering me jobs. And Jordan's father said I was extraordinary. Do you believe that? And I just got an idea that could maybe help me stay here."

I crept over to the door that led downstairs and heard my mother still pawing through boxes of books.

"If Mom was interested in somebody, she wouldn't want to move back east, right? So all I have to do is help her find somebody to date here in West Paradise. And I'm thinking about Larry Deluxe, this guy she met tonight."

I stopped talking, listened again, picked up the phone.

"God, if you knew Larry, you would know what a desperate character you're talking to here. I'm about to sell my mother down the river for a few months in West Paradise! I gotta go. Talk to you later."

I found a classical station on the radio and turned it on,

snatched two emergency candles out of the cupboard, couldn't find the holders, but lit them anyway.

Then I poured myself some juice, sat at the counter, and tried to look casual as I flipped through the newspaper.

Mom stood in the doorway of the living room, a book in her hand. "Tony!"

"What?"

"Why are the lights off?"

"Um, I've got a headache. Light hurts my eyes."

She groped for the switch. "What are these candles doing on the couch?"

"I couldn't find the holders."

"So you stuck lighted candles between the cushions? Are you insane?"

"They're tall. They aren't going to catch anything on fire."

She blew them out and fanned at the smoke. She put *Getting What You Deserve* on the coffee table. "Go to bed, Tony."

"I just want to finish this article. It's interesting."

"Go to bed, Tony."

"It's about killer bees. They're due in Washington, D.C., right after the holidays. The article says nobody should even think about moving to the East Coast."

She pointed upstairs.

"Can't I even say good-night to Larry?"

"Go!"

I went, but not as far as she wanted me to.

"All the way," she shouted. "In your room and close the door."

So I ran water in the sink and flushed the toilet. Then I sat at my desk and waited. I heard Larry come in. I gave them a few minutes, then turned off the light and opened my door a crack. The big hum sorted itself out: "Four husbands . . . only Tony and I." "Kate . . . interesting . . . half a dozen experts on stuff like that."

Opening my door wider, I crept into the hall, past the guest room and the bath, right to the edge of the landing. I could see them a little, but they couldn't see me at all.

"Is that wine okay?" Larry asked. "I got it from a sponsor."

"I don't usually drink. It just makes me sad."

"Really? Still?"

"Well, sometimes," Mom said with an edge, "sadness is appropriate."

"Don't disagree with him," I muttered.

"Well, it's a matter of degree, isn't it, Kate? Most of those grief books want you on your feet and working in six months. I kind of remember one of the exercises tells you to sob fifteen minutes a day. But only fifteen minutes."

"How do you know that?"

I mouthed the first six words right along with him: "I did a show on it. When I was in Houston. Had some grief hotshots on a conference call."

I saw her squirm on the couch. "But I've lost four husbands."

He shrugged. "So you should know the drill."

"You don't understand."

"You're not the first person to tell me that, and I'm sure it hasn't been easy for you, but the fact is . . ."

Mom stood up. "I'll show you how easy it hasn't been. Follow me." And she headed for the door to the den.

Larry got to his feet. "Are we going downstairs? I had an Egyptologist on once who claimed every time we descend we call on Osiris."

Mom went, "This is serious now."

He reached for the bottle. "I'd better bring the wine then.

And I'm leaving that negotiation book of yours right here where I won't forget it."

When they disappeared, I tiptoed downstairs. He'd left the door open, so I could hear a little, but not much. I knew if I wasn't careful, they might see me. So I got down on all fours and put my head through the door like a wary cat.

"It's of Bill's birthday party," Mom explained, and I heard the old VCR whir and click.

"Bill was number four, right?"

Slithering headfirst down the carpeted stair, I saw Larry's wineglass point to the screen with its familiar scenes: the partygoers in their pointy hats, men in Dockers, women wearing sandals, most everybody with drinks in their hands, and literally everybody in a line putting their left or right whatever in and shaking it all about.

"That's Bill," Mom said. "In the white shirt."

Larry wagged his big head. "What'd he do for a living?"

"Sold insurance."

"And the ones before?"

"Well, Tony's father was the ambassador from Panama, Dennis owned and operated his own tug on the Mississippi, and Russ wrote novels about the Southwest."

"Amazing. One of those experts I was telling you about? She said that women with bad luck like yours hedge their bets after a while."

With my nose buried in the carpet, I muttered, "Easy, Larry."

He drained his glass and poured another. "And look at you: an ambassador could get shot, a river pilot could get hurt. So next time you pick a guy who sits at home in front of a word processor and tells stories. Even that doesn't work, so you go right to the one who knows the most about probability, Mr. Actuarial himself—an insurance man."

Mom ran one hand across her forehead. "I never thought about it like that."

"You should marry me. Nothing ever happens to me."

"Yes!" I hissed. Bracing myself—one hand on the wall, one on the first little rung of the miniature banister—I oozed down one more step.

I could see a little better and I liked what I saw. Mom's hand reached for Larry's. "Here," she said, staring at the screen and cringing.

I could hear everything now, including the complete sound track. "You put your left foot in," everyone sang, "you put your left foot out."

"The hokey-pokey?" Larry leaned forward. "Not exactly the Philosophers' Ball, is it."

Mom's right hand covered her mouth. "Oh, God," she muttered.

Larry sang along. He got up and joined in. He shook his left arm. He shook his right arm.

Mom started to sniffle. The music told me that Bill was crumpling to the ground. I saw Larry lean right into the screen. I tried to relax one strained, quivering arm as he shouted, "Man, that is something! If I had a TV show, I could do an hour on Women Whose Husbands Died Dancing. We start with the tango, end with the hokey-pokey."

"Larry!" I muttered into the rug. "Shut up and hold her hand."

Mom slid to the other end of the couch. "I wanted you to see this because I'm sick and tired of people like you telling me how I ought to feel. Four men I loved died. I've watched Bill die a hundred times on this tape and it doesn't get any easier. And it certainly isn't funny."

Larry looked at his shoes. "I guess what I'm trying to say is it's not funny that he died. It's funny *how* he died."

128

"I don't believe there's anything funny about—"

"I had a guy on the air once who told me that life was desperate but not serious. I guess I kind of feel that way, too."

"If you ask me, it's both desperate and—"

Larry interrupted her. "Do you think Bill would want you to still feel bad?"

"Well, no, but . . ."

Larry started to bob his head and sing, "You put your left foot in . . ." Then he started to dance. "You put your left foot out. You put your left foot in, and you shake it . . ."

All of a sudden he clutched his chest, then collapsed. I mean really collapsed. He didn't crumple or slump; he hit the floor with a splat.

Mom leaped to her feet. "Larry!"

He got right back up. "Nope. False alarm. Not dead yet."

"Larry, stop this."

He turned around. "You put your big head in, you put your big head out . . ." He grabbed his shirt again, this time with both hands. Down he went.

"Are you insane?" Mom shouted.

"Is that a little smile I see, Kathryn?"

"No!"

Larry pushed himself up onto his knees and shuffled toward her like someone doing serious penance. "I think I saw a little smile." Then he shot to his feet. "Do it with me: you put your bootie in, you put your bootie out."

Mom struggled, but he wouldn't let go of her hands. I saw her little smile get bigger, then turn into a grin.

"That's it!" cried Larry. "That's what Bill would want."

When he let her go, she collapsed onto the couch, laughing and crying at the same time. Which made me start to laugh, partly because Larry was so outrageous, partly because I hadn't seen Mom really laugh for a long time and I was relieved, partly because she seemed to like him!

But I couldn't do all of that and hold on, too. The foot I had hooked in the door slipped, my arms gave out, and I slid headfirst downstairs like a package on a chute and ended up in a ball at the foot of the stairs.

They stared down at me; I stared up at them. Finally I said, "Are you sure nobody wants coffee?"

~~~~

Next morning I crept into the kitchen. Mom was sitting at the counter, a half-eaten bagel in front of her. Instead of a nightgown, she had on a rose-colored silk blouse and brown linen slacks.

She glanced up at me, then back down to the half-open newspaper in front of her. She didn't say anything; I didn't say anything. But we both acted like people in a house where the baby is sleeping: I only opened the refrigerator a few inches, the pages of her newspaper barely fluttered. I poured juice down the side of my glass so it wouldn't go glug-glug and then decided on oatmeal, the world's most silent cereal.

In that atmosphere, the whir of a microwave was like a lawn mower, but she didn't twitch, and neither did I. When my oatmeal was done, I dipped into the center of the bowl, rather than risk the slightest clink with my spoon.

"Nice to see you on your feet," she said finally, "instead of rolling down the stairs."

"You shouldn't have sent me to my room," I muttered without looking up. "I'm too old to be sent upstairs like some little kid."

She whipped off her reading glasses. "You were acting like a child, sneaking around like that. It reminded me of when you used to play crocodile. Remember crocodile? You slithered

130

everywhere and I had to put your lunch on the floor. That may have been fine when you were four, but not . . ."

I stood up. "I wasn't playing crocodile or anything else. I was just . . . well, I was just interested in what was going to happen."

"My God, I've raised a Peeping Tom."

"Not like that. I just wanted to know if you guys were getting along."

"In heaven's name, why?"

I wiped my palms on my jeans like I was just about to try to lift a Volkswagen. "Because I like it here."

"Where?"

"Here. In West Paradise."

"And what's Larry got to do with that?"

"Well, I thought maybe that if you liked him, maybe you'd stay for a while." I saw her frown, so I talked faster. "And what's not to like? He made you laugh last night. When's the last time you laughed like that?"

She squeezed my hand. "Sweetie, he did make me laugh, and I slept straight through last night without one pill; but I could never think of Larry as anything more than a friend, and this place goes on the market in January."

"It isn't the only condo in town."

She narrowed her eyes. "This is mostly about Jordan, isn't it? Not just the stately elms of West Paradise."

"A little. But it's about everything. I like it here; I've got friends. Drew Archer likes me. Somebody offered me a job prepping for a really famous chef." I stepped closer and took one of her cold hands. "Just stay till June. Let me finish a school year someplace that means something to me."

Mom angled me toward the counter and the two stools. "Tony, honey. There are a lot of issues here. Including finances and getting back to Washington, where I've still got a few connections that could lead to a job. And, anyway, whatever happens, Larry Deluxe isn't going to have anything to do with it." She pushed me back onto the bar stool. "Even though I'm going to be working for him."

That got my attention. "What? That's great."

"It's not great; it's business. And it won't last long."

I tried to act casual. "So how'd this happen?"

"Well, last night out on the porch as I was apologizing for you, he suggested I act as his agent. For that contract negotiation we were talking about."

"Cool."

"It isn't cool. It's business, and it could be finished next week. KGAB is offering forty thousand dollars. I told Larry I'd helped Russ with his contracts and thought I could help him, too. He said I could have ten percent of anything over forty."

"You can get way over forty. Absolutely."

"So the soft music and the candles that could have set the couch on fire were your way of fixing me up with Larry."

"That was even before I knew he could make you laugh."

She picked invisible lint off her slacks. "I merely think he's undervalued."

"See?"

"Not by me, Tony. By the conglomerate that owns KGAB. He's good at what he does. He got me talking. I didn't plan on telling him about Bill; I sure didn't plan on showing him that tape; I'm through with that tape. But we started looking at the negotiation book, and he's asking me about this and that and the next thing you know . . ."

"Exactly, he's easy to talk to."

"Will you relax?"

She crossed the room, leaving behind a whiff of perfume, and pried open the miniblinds. "He just pulled up." Then she turned toward me. "Tell him you're sorry for eavesdropping, okay?"

"Sure."

She opened the door wide, stood in it, and waved. Larry bounded up the steps. He was wearing brown slacks with a stain, a white shirt with a stain, and his hair looked like he'd slept standing on his head.

While they were still shaking hands like she'd just bought a car, Mom said, "Tony wants to apologize for last night."

He glanced my way. "Hey, Tony, I'll have that coffee now."

I blushed. "I really am sorry. I shouldn't have been snooping around like that."

"Forget it. Hey, that gives me an idea for a show about snooping, you know? Who snoops, why people snoop, snooping through the ages, the future of snooping, troupes of snoopers, should you shoot a snooper, the loot that snoopers root for, the—"

"Larry, stop!" Mom sounded like she was training a cocker spaniel.

"Sorry. But would you be on, Tony? Get the teen angle on things?"

Mom rolled her eyes as I said, "I'd love to be on. Especially in June."

"Can I just use your bathroom?" Larry asked. "I need to wash up. I overslept."

"Upstairs, second door on the left."

From the landing, he shouted down, "Oh, Kate? I'm having all my calls forwarded here, okay? In case negotiations heat up."

When we heard the bathroom door close, she looked at me. "It's just a job," she said. "And it's not going to last very long."

"Then stay for me," I blurted. "Just because I asked you to."

"Sweetie, it's not that easy. Aunt Polly is making some arrangements in Washington and—"

"Can't she make 'em for June instead of January?"

Mom frowned. "Why are you like this all of a sudden?"

"Like what?"

"Difficult."

"I'm difficult? You should talk. All I'm doing is asking you for a few more months here than we planned. One thing."

Just then the phone rang. "Can we talk about this later?"

"Are we really going to talk about it, or have you already made up your mind."

She frowned at me as she picked up the receiver. "Mr. Deluxe is indisposed right now. May I ask who's calling? Just a moment." She put her hand over the receiver, the receiver to her heart. "This isn't like you."

"Maybe it's not," I yelled on my way out the door, "but maybe it should be."

There was a phone next to the Shell station on Jericho Street, but I didn't want to talk to a machine. I wanted to see Jordan.

〰〰〰

At W.P.H.S. I cut between buildings. Barry's henchmen were watching their idol. He strolled up to a crowd of girls wearing sweatshirts with cuddly bears on them and said something. Then they all screamed and backed away.

I made myself nod to a couple of people, then spotted Hector cruising my way wearing a cowboy hat and, propped on the footrests of his chair, black boots.

"I need something shocking for the Frost Ogre to do," he said, frowning down at his sketchbook.

"Has he got a mother?"

"Actually, yeah."

"Maybe he could freeze her to death."

He took a good look at me. "You okay, man?"

Just then Jordan and Blue came around the corner. She was wearing painter's pants, a T-shirt, and . . . oh, my God. This time she'd really outdone herself: two tiny dart boards and, in each one, three darts clustered in the bull's-eye.

I looked at Hector. "She can't get away with that bra at school, can she?"

Just then she caught sight of me and shouted, "Tony! Come here!"

I met her halfway. She put her arms around my neck and kissed me.

"I didn't know friends kissed friends like that," I said. And I kissed back.

"I'm so glad to see you."

"Me, too."

That's when Barry showed up. "Jordan, babe. Cool bra. Makes me want to score." As he leered, Jordan stepped away from me, arched her back, and stuck out her chest—what there was of it.

"Take a good look," she said. "These darts are what it feels like to have someone like you ogle my boobs five days of the week."

Barry looked baffled, almost hurt as he frowned and said, "Huh?"

Before she could answer, Ms. Christophe rushed up.

"What do you think you're doing, Jordan?" she asked.

"Something that I hope will make Barry think twice before he unleashes that bozo consciousness around here."

"Well," Ms. Christophe said coldly, "it's totally inappropriate and distasteful to the administration."

Jordan stepped back. "I don't think you understand. I'm not the one who's wrong here."

"Jordan, school is not a forum for this kind of personal statement."

"Yeah? Well, why is it a forum for guys to look down every girl's shirt? You think that's not their personal statements?"

"Don't make things worse, Jordan," she warned. "Just take that ridiculous contraption off and go to your homeroom."

Jordan scanned the growing crowd. "You want me," she said loud enough for everybody to hear, "to take off my bra? Is that right?"

Ms. Christophe glanced around uneasily. "I'm asking you to stop disrupting things." Then she stepped closer. "C'mon, Jordan. You and I have always gotten along."

"You come on," Jordan hissed back. "I've got some legal rights here."

Ms. Christophe pointed to Barry. "Do you think that he would have approached you like he did if he hadn't been encouraged by your outfit?"

Jordan looked amazed. "*I* made Barry disgusting? Barry's always been disgusting."

"By your actions and demeanor you encouraged him to—"

"Are you saying I asked to be harassed?"

Ms. Christophe was lecturing now. "Actions that disrupt other students cannot and will not be condoned, much less encouraged."

"What do you think *his* actions are? You think it's not disruptive to have guys always—"

"Please take that thing off and come with me."

Jordan retreated, both hands raised protectively. Then she

pulled herself together and stepped back up to within inches of Ms. Christophe. "I'm not going anywhere."

"You realize what you're forcing me to do, don't you?"

I could see where this was going, and it made me nervous. "Wait a minute," I said. "Everybody take a break here. There's gotta be another way to settle this."

"Like what?" said Blue. "Waiting for the Establishment to appoint a committee to study the problem? No way."

"I didn't say anything about a school board. I just think . . ."

Ms. Christophe put one hand on my shoulder. "Stay out of this, Tony." She turned to Jordan. "One last chance: take that vulgar thing off or you're suspended."

Jordan pointed to her creation. "This isn't vulgar. This is about *his* vulgarity!"

Ms. Christophe's jaw was tight. "Be reasonable, Jordan. You were reasonable when I asked you to keep your Confess-O-Rama posters off campus. Be reasonable about this."

All of a sudden I couldn't breathe. I looked at Jordan. "You're Confess-O-Rama?" I couldn't believe it. "That means . . ."

"Relax, Tony," Jordan said. "One thing at a time here."

Ms. Christophe crossed her arms. "One last chance, Jordan."

Jordan crossed her arms. "I'm not taking anything off."

"Then you're suspended." Ms. Christophe fished for her referral slips. "And," she announced, "she might not be the only one if I don't see people heading for their homerooms soon."

Jordan was Confess-O-Rama. Oh, my God.

A lot of other kids were watching, and when Blue and Hector and Jordan headed for the street, they came along, too, kind of in an undertow. Stunned, I staggered after them.

"Barry?" Jordan shouted. "Can you get a hold of your

dad? This is censorship! Wasn't he going to do a show about that?"

I hurried up beside her and hissed, "Let me get this straight: it was you I was spilling my guts to?"

She lurched away. "It's not like that."

"Yeah? Well, what is it like?"

Gunslinger-style, Barry whipped a phone out of one pocket. "I'll page him. You and I could go on the air together, do pro and con like 'Firing Line.' "

"Just call him."

Ms. Christophe had followed Jordan, and a couple dozen kids had followed her.

"Completely off campus," she bellowed. "I mean it."

Deliberately Jordan stepped into the street, then looked up at Barry, Blue, Hector, Rochelle. Looked at everybody but me. "We need bodies. I want a rally tomorrow, and a rally's no good without lots and lots of people." She hopped up on the curb just long enough to appeal to everybody behind us. "And it needs to be visual. It needs to look good on TV news."

I walked right up to her again, almost as close as when we'd kissed. "You set me up to use my secrets in some art piece?"

She leaned toward me. "I didn't set you up. You know me: I'm always late, I'm always disorganized. So I didn't listen to the tapes until last night. That's when I got to know the Tony I wanted to kiss. You were so honest and open. I loved it!"

Blue butted in. "What about robots? Symbols of mindless authority."

"Lots of black," Hector chimed in. "For the death of freedom of expression."

I pulled her farther away. "All those nights with me sitting

138

on the floor," I said, "thinking I'm talking to a machine, and it turns out to be you!"

"What's so terrible about that? We're friends. All you were doing is telling stuff to a friend."

"When were you going to tell me that you knew?"

"Tony, the show's only . . ."

"You weren't, were you? You were going to wait and see if I'd call a few more times."

"Tony, it's art. It's for art's sake. That makes it different."

"For you, maybe. Not for me."

Blue loped over to us again. "Jordan, what if we—"

She waved him away. "Just a minute, Blue! Tony, try and understand. Am I mad that you said I had bony knees and my hair stood up funny? Am I mad that you kept calling me weird?"

I started backing away.

"Hey, I didn't make you call," she shouted after me. "I didn't twist your arm! It's not all my fault."

"What's the problem?" Blue asked as I stormed by him.

"None of your business."

He grabbed at my T-shirt. "Hey, whatever it is, it's just personal. And that's not going to be as important as Jordan's . . ."

I pulled away from him, then turned around to leave. "Don't tell me what's important and what's not, Blue."

The last thing I heard was Ms. Christophe. "Away from the school, Jordan. I mean it now."

I headed off in the other direction, knowing I couldn't go home because Mom was there.

Five minutes later, I was waiting for the bus that would take me uptown when I saw the pay phone. There was nobody around except an old lady dozing on the bench, so

I went over and without putting any money in, just held the receiver like I was used to doing.

"What do I do now," I shouted, "except get out of this stupid town as fast as I can."

〰〰〰

Next morning I slunk downstairs to find Mom hunched over the counter, reading glasses perched on her nose. She took them off when she saw me, and folded them deliberately, like she was about to hand down a Supreme Court decision.

"This has got to stop," she said. "I have had the cold shoulder since I got home last night." She grabbed for my wrist when I tried to sneak past. "Why won't you tell me what's wrong? Is it still that business about staying in West Paradise? I said we could talk it over, and I meant it."

"It's not that."

"Is it something at school?"

"Just leave me alone."

"No. That's what I'd tell you when I'd cried till my nightgown was wet. And you'd fix some soup and make me get out of bed. I didn't mean it then, and you don't mean it now."

I leaned against the refrigerator. I looked around the kitchen. *My* kitchen. "Okay, maybe you're right. There is something." Just then the phone rang. I watched her listen.

"You may talk to me," she said. "I'm Kathryn Candelaria, Larry's agent."

She started to revolve in the kitchen, waving her free hand, wrapping herself in the long cord like I'd done when I was blabbing to you-know-who.

"Who's bluffing. Nobody is bluffing; it's a reasonable request. What do you plan to do, start playing 'The Best of Larry Deluxe'? Good as they are, that'll get old pretty fast."

I picked up my book bag and angled for the door.

"This is not a good day. If there was any way we could put our meeting off until . . ." She waved me back. When I was in grabbing distance, she grabbed me, put one arm around me.

"Well, I haven't heard of you, either," she said. "So we're even. And if I have to come today, I will. There are flights from Burbank just about every hour."

She leaned over and tried to kiss me on the cheek, but I pulled away.

"I'm going to have to call you back," she said into the phone. "I've got someone from Pacifica Radio on the other line. I'll just be a second."

She looked flustered, mussed, and excited as she said, "Honey, I'm going to fly to San Francisco this morning, but I'll be back before you're home from school. We'll talk then, I promise."

"Wait a minute. You wanted to know what's wrong; I want to tell you what's wrong. I'm sick of West Paradise."

She followed me to the door. "What? What are you talking about? Yesterday you were mad because we weren't staying here." She followed me down the walk. "Tony? What's going on?"

A couple of blocks away was a park, so I sat there kind of half-hidden in the bushes like a pervert until Mom drove by on her way to the airport. Then I went back home.

I ran water in the sink, plunged both hands in, splashed my face. Rolling up my sleeves, I got out my cutting board and knives.

What a relief to slice, sauté, and handle, braise, tear, pour, measure; to open the avocado, thwack the seed with a shiny blade, and twist it free of the perfect, green, boat-shaped half; to spin the lettuce dry and let it tumble into the bowl blue as a turquoise crater; to look at the silver, orderly in its drawer, the light off each knife and fork, the spoons tucked together on their sides the way Jordan and I had dozed in the sun one afternoon when she couldn't work anymore and she called up crying and I went over and calmed her down.

∿∿∿

When the chicken was so tender it slipped from the bone, I spooned some onto the plate. The salad glistened, the tall glass of milk was an ivory column. I looked at the single folded napkin, one knife, fork, and spoon, one plate, one chair pulled out. One of everything.

At school, probably hundreds of kids were dressed for the rally, milling around, waiting for it to happen. Hector would be there and Blue and Rochelle. And Jordan.

Just then the doorbell rang.

Larry Deluxe was wearing jeans and a T-shirt with his picture on it. "What are you doing here, Tony?"

"Me? What are *you* doing here?"

"Your mom called from the airport. She had a feeling I should stop by. Why aren't you in school?"

I sat down with a thud. "Why aren't *you* at school? I thought you'd be the emcee or the moderator or something."

"What there is to moderate. Anyway, I've got time, especially since your mom thought she could do better in San Francisco without me." Nose up, sniffing, he glided toward the kitchen. "What smells good?"

"Chicken cacciatore."

"For breakfast?"

"I just wanted to cook. It didn't matter what. Cooking calms me down."

"What have you got to be upset about?"

"Nothing. None of your business."

142

He lifted a lid, stuck one finger in the sauce, then licked it. "That's right. You cooked stuff for Jordan's party, didn't you."

"It wasn't just Jordan's party; it was her dad's, too." And mine.

"So, she's not coming over later to eat this?"

"No."

"Is that why you're home, you had a fight with Jordan? And is that why you weren't at Jordan's last night helping to get ready for the rally?"

"None of your business."

He looked into the skillet again. "I'm starved. This looks great; why not eat it? Set me a place, okay?"

"Set your own place."

He opened cabinets until he found a plate. I watched him pile lettuce on it, then cover that with chicken and sauce.

I shook my head. "It's not a casserole. You're never going to taste anything."

He took a forkful and chewed. "I'm used to eating alone, I guess. Oh, man, this is good, though." He tapped on my plate with a fork. "You eat, too. Your mom worries about you." He shook his head. "You both worry about each other entirely, and I mean entirely, too much."

"You never worried about your folks?"

He held out one hand and made that wobbly little-of-this-little-of-that motion. "It was different for me. Nobody kept dying. Anyway, when I was your age, I was on the road selling anything and everything."

"You never graduated from high school?"

"Nope. I mean, I went to adult ed and got my diploma when I was twenty something, but no cap and gown, no reunions where they all say, 'Why, look. It's Larry Dingle.'"

"Your name is Dingle?"

"Yeah, but picture that on a T-shirt."

"Or worse—shorts."

Larry laughed. "We could have used some humor last night at the big sign-painting shindig. Everything's just Down with Censorship. And it wasn't that big a shindig, anyway. But you're not interested in that. Let's eat some more salad."

I gave him some. "This is so good," he raved, chewing with his mouth open. "Why is this so good?"

"Well, everything's fresh and the bowl's been seasoned and what time's the rally?"

"Noon."

I looked at the clock. "It's getting kind of late."

He crammed more romaine into his mouth. "Let me worry about that. Since when have you been into this food thing?"

"As our friends the Native Americans might say—two husbands ago."

"You know, you're a really good cook."

"I just cook sometimes. I'm not a cook."

"Sure you are. This chicken cacciatore is great. And so was that potato salad and all that other stuff of yours at the party."

"It was okay."

He leaned toward me, one hand swooping across the table to land on my shoulder. "Does cooking make you happy?"

"I guess."

"And you're good at it?"

"I guess."

"And you like food, right?"

"Sure."

"So you're a cook. Or should be. I had Wolfgang Puck on once. Or was that Julia Child. Anyway, it was somebody in a tall, white hat. Just say the word and I'll get you into chef's school." He swept the palm of one hand across the air. "I can see it now. Big neon sign that says Tony's Place."

"That's original."

He took another handful of salad and plopped it onto my plate. "Eat with me. I might eat alone a lot, but I don't like it."

I gave myself a little of everything as Larry chewed intently, regularly forking lettuce in. Then he stopped, pushed his plate away, and took a deep breath, letting his chest expand. "This is kind of nice. I'm glad you were home, even if it's a school day. Even if your reason for being here's a big fat secret."

"Okay, okay. I'm home because Jordan and I had a fight. All right?"

"Like I didn't guess."

"You wouldn't believe what she did."

"Talk to me."

"No way." I pushed some chicken around on my plate. I took a bite of salad. "Talking's what got me into this!"

He shot to his feet. "In the car then. There's nothing like men-in-cars. Makes for instant intimacy and bonding."

"Who said?"

"The guy who wrote *Men in Cars: Instant Intimacy and Bonding*."

"Why didn't I guess that?"

"C'mon."

I leaned across the table for his plate. "Just let me—"

He slapped my hand. Hard. "No. That's not the way it works. You cooked, you don't clean up, too. When we come back, I'll clean up. Sound fair?"

"Let me at least put some of this stuff in the refrigerator so it won't spoil."

"Okay, and then you drive." He tossed me the keys.

I stared at them. His key chain had a plastic holder with

145

a picture of Sheila Larson in it. She looked up at me from my hand. "But I don't know how . . ."

"Yeah, you do. All guys know how to drive. It's in our DNA. Now put that chicken away and get behind the wheel."

"All I've got is a learner's permit."

"So we're set. Anyway, I know all the cops in Paradise. Nothin's going to happen."

A couple of minutes later I followed him down the walk, then settled into the stained gray seat.

"Look, this is nice of you, but—"

"Put the key in." He folded both arms behind his head. "*Turn* the key," he said patiently. As the Dodge started to shudder, he ordered, "Let's drive past the radio station so they'll see I'm not worried."

I slid the shift lever into *D*, then pulled—oozed, really—away from the curb.

"See!" he said triumphantly.

"I watched Mom," I admitted. " 'Cause I was afraid I might have to get her to the hospital or someplace in a hurry. And then, you know, I practiced in the driveway a couple of times." I swallowed hard; Larry's car felt a lot different from our Subaru. "I won't go fast or anything."

He frowned. "C'mon, you're not with Mommy now."

I sped up, a little anyway, until I got to the red light, where I had to hit the brakes. The car rocked, but he didn't say anything. Then I heard a faint voice. "Larry, how come I can hear you on the radio and see you, too?"

His window cranked halfway down and stuck. "The magic of tape, sweetheart."

"Stereo Larrys. I like it."

The light turned green, and the Jetta convertible sped away. The woman who was driving waved without looking back.

"That's why I went to Houston." Larry sounded depressed all of a sudden.

I peered down the nearly empty street. "Her?"

"Somebody like her. It was stupid; anyway, what with Sheila mad and jealous and all, Texas looked a lot better than Paradise." He glanced over at me. "You're not being stupid about Jordan, are you?"

I was stopped at a corner. There was nobody else in either direction, so I just stayed there.

Finally I blurted, "Jordan is Confess-O-Rama."

"What is that supposed to mean?"

"You didn't see those fliers all over town? Call Confess-O-Rama and spill your guts? Jordan *is* Confess-O-Rama."

"Oh, those. Yeah, I called, left a message, said I wanted to do a show on it. Nobody ever got back to me. So that was Jordan's idea?"

"For the art show next week."

"Sounds like her. So?"

"So I called this machine and spilled my guts. I was talking to her about her!"

"Like what did you tell it?"

"*Her.* I told *her* that she was the kind of girl who'd wear a road pizza wrist corsage and another time I told her that she's not the kind of girl I'd ever go out with and another time I told her that I liked her a lot and I was so desperate to stay in West Paradise that I was going to try and fix Mom . . ." *up with Larry Deluxe.* Whoops.

"What?" Larry asked. "Fix Mom what?"

We glided by a coffee shop. "Uh, a meat loaf."

Larry rubbed his jaw thoughtfully. "Let me get this straight: you don't want to move, your mom does, but she'll stay once you fix her a meat loaf?" He looked over at me. "You *are* a good cook."

"Larry, the point is that Jordan should have told me that she was Confess-O-Rama. Right from the beginning she should have told me."

He shrugged. "Maybe. Probably."

"Probably nothing. She let me make a fool out of myself. And she would've kept letting me make a fool out of myself, too."

"So she betrayed you in a way, right?"

"Exactly. She betrayed me."

"But why?"

When somebody behind me honked, I turned left. "She said it was for art's sake."

Larry linked both hands behind his head, as if he were relaxing in a hammock. "That's probably true. Artists are different from you and me. Also I'll bet she liked hearing you let your hair down. In person you're a little standoffish, a little shut down . . ."

"Me, shut down?"

"Tony, my friend, you're kind of a quip *meister*, but that's not the same as being open."

I looked down at the grimy steering wheel and muttered, "She did start to say something about me being honest and vulnerable. But I just split."

"Understandable. You were mad. But, what we're doing now is almost Confess-O-Rama, right? You're telling me stuff you wouldn't tell everybody. What's the difference?"

"The difference is I know who I'm talking to *and* you aren't going to tell anybody else."

"I'm on the radio, remember?"

"You wouldn't . . ."

"How's she going to use all this delicious dirt, anyhow? I mean, are you the only one in the piece? Is there a big picture

148

on it, like with you in your underpants and a sign saying FIVE CENTS TO HEAR THE BONEHEAD TALK?"

I swung so wide around a corner that Larry grabbed for the wheel. "I guess I can't be the only one," I admitted.

"Right. So she's going to use a little of what you said in her art and the rest she's going to keep in her heart." He grinned at me. "Hey, that rhymed. That was good."

I concentrated on the street for a little while. "She still shouldn't have done it."

"I agree. But that's past history."

"All history is past, Larry. That's why it's history."

"You're kidding." He scratched his head as, all of a sudden, I pounded on the steering wheel with both fists.

"She made me so mad!"

"Do you think she still likes you?"

"For what she can get out of me, maybe. As long as I keep talking."

"Did she say that?"

"Well, no. She said that after hearing the tapes she wanted to kiss me." I took a deep breath. "But why would she want to kiss somebody like me? Man, instead of Confess-O-Rama I should've been dialing 1-800-*PITIFUL.*"

Larry shook me gently. "Hey, don't be so hard on yourself. She listened to you be honest as hell about all kinds of things, so now she knows a lot about you and she still wants to kiss you."

I concentrated on driving. I went a little faster. I took one hand off the wheel. Finally I admitted, "I guess I didn't say anything really bad."

"So, even more reason to let her use a few words of it for her art piece." Larry leaned toward me. "Tell me this," he said. "Once you talked to that machine, probably late at night, right? By yourself in the dark, right? Once you said whatever you said, weren't you glad you'd done it?"

I thought back to those times on the phone. How I'd go upstairs feeling, I don't know, lighter somehow. Even if I was confused or upset.

"Okay, okay, but she—"

"Then you ought to thank Jordan. Because without Confess-O-Rama you're still putting a lid on it and working on an ulcer. By the way, you're not still mad at her, are you?"

"A little."

"You know what they say—forgive and forgive."

"That's forgive and forget."

"Even better."

Larry turned on the radio, listened to himself for a few seconds, then turned it off.

I just stared at him, shaking my head slowly.

"What now?" Larry asked.

"Man, you are the last person I ever thought I'd be talking to about this."

"We should do a show on that, you know? Call it Unlikely Confidants. Or maybe I've already done a show on it and that's why it sounds like a good idea." He upended a bottle of water he'd found on the floor.

"Drew Archer said to look for help from an unlikely source."

"Really? He is such a weird cat." He glanced at his watch. "Hey, it's getting a little late. And I promised that I'd do dishes. So point this rocket ship toward home."

〰〰〰

Larry and I stood at the sink together. Neither one of us said very much; we just did the work. He'd wash something, hand it to me, and I'd dry it and put it away.

150

"Do you want the radio on?" I asked.

"No, I get plenty of radio."

So we stood there listening to what I guess you might call the music of domesticity: the ping of silverware, the swish of sponge, the gong of skillet and lid.

"I'll be careful," he said, slowly submerging my good pan last. "This looks like a nice one."

Larry swept suds down the drain while I folded the dish towels and hung them on their rack. Then we grinned at each other.

He leaned toward the door. "Maybe after the rally I'll go home and clean up my own kitchen. That'd be different." He led me to the foyer. "Nice morning," he said. "Don't tell Sly Stallone, but I really liked doing dishes with you."

I grinned back and shook his hand, still warm from the water. "Yeah, me, too."

He stepped out onto the little porch. "See you later. After the rally, maybe."

"You think I should go, don't you."

He turned around so he could look right at me. "It could turn out to be kind of a bust. Blue was saying last night that he asks kids to for sure show up, and they say things like, 'I talked to my folks, and they say not to get involved.' Or, 'Ms. Christophe's right.' Or my favorite: 'A black armband would like clash with my new sweater.'"

"Yeah, but what could I do?"

"Just show up."

"And swell the crowd from four to five?"

"Tony, Jordan needs you. You're not just another body. You're her boyfriend." He took a step backward. "Look, I gotta split."

I watched him walk away. I could read his slumped shoulders like they were a sign saying THINK IT OVER, TONY. Then

151

I got an idea, a good idea but one that made me real jittery real fast.

I dashed inside and rummaged through kitchen drawers for twine, a stapler, and some duct tape. Then I opened the refrigerator, reached into the vegetable crisper, took out what I wanted, laid everything on the counter, took a deep breath, and went to work.

~~~~

Twenty minutes later, I hurried through West Paradise. People were walking their perfect dogs. All the old folks strolled around thinking their grandchildren were cuter than anybody else's and smiling like they had made good investments their whole lives. A mom pushed her twins in a carriage that probably cost more than Larry's car.

At school, a couple of frowning mothers leaned on their Volvos, arms crossed. One of them pointed to the rickety three-tiered risers and a battered reel-to-reel tape machine, probably Larry's on-site studio.

I looked down at the huge shirt I'd thrown on: *Oh, man.*

There were a lot of kids milling around, but most of them gave the makeshift stage a wide berth. Maybe a dozen people carried DOWN WITH CENSORSHIP signs. Only Blue was dressed like a robot, and Rochelle—all in black—marched behind Hector, who carried a sign that said CENSORSHIP CRIPPLES! That was pretty much it. That was the rally.

Standing on the steps of the Administration Building were Ms. Christophe and the mysterious Mr. Emery, a guy with one of those quarter-moon faces—pushed in the middle, a pointy chin and forehead. He turned toward his assistant-principal and said something as Barry, holding a giant boom box broadcasting a supersolemn Gregorian chant, pulled up at the curb ahead of us and hopped off the trunk of somebody's Ford.

Jordan climbed out of the backseat. She wore a loose white smock buttoned over camouflage fatigues. A handkerchief, barely whiter than her face, covered her mouth. Both hands were tied behind her back.

As I tugged at my floppy shirt, Jordan fell in behind Hector, who'd rolled over to meet her at the curb.

A clump of kids made a path for them, a wide one, like somebody was contagious. Barry's carton-size Sony bled the somber chant out into the noontime haze as Jordan climbed the three steps, turned, and faced the spectators. I watched Barry motion for his father; then he shot to the stage and grabbed the mike.

"Ladies and gentlemen," he bellowed. "Put your hands together for the king of Paradise talk radio and the man behind the myth. A big round of applause for"—here his voice got husky and ultrasincere—"my father!"

Larry bounded up onto the top step. Jordan just stood there pale as a communion candle. I started to drift toward the stage, slipping between people, waiting for a surge or ebb, oozing through here, sliding there. Some kids didn't even notice. A few nudged their pals and pointed at me.

"What's going on?" somebody asked.

Somebody answered. "Jordan Archer's doing something."

"I heard she wants to get rid of Saturday school!"

"I heard she got suspended for taking her bra off."

"I heard she threw darts at Barry Deluxe."

When Larry picked up the microphone, it made those weird, extraterrestrial yodels. He jumped back, then lifted it to his mouth carefully, like it was an onion ice-cream cone.

"Folks, uh, thanks for coming." He motioned for everybody to step closer, but almost nobody did. "This is going to be a live tape-delay broadcast, so you can hear yourselves at three o'clock today, and then there'll be a call-in segment."

It was a weird scene: Blue, Rochelle, and Hector stood right in front of the stage. A few yards behind them were the kids holding the signs, but not even up in the air. They moved them up and down slowly, like they were churning butter. Behind them—a long way behind them—stood everybody else. Those kids could hear what Larry said, but they weren't really listening. They were there, but not there, like people gaping at an accident on the freeway—curious but not curious enough to stop and help.

"I've been wondering," Larry said, straightening up, "about what a school is supposed to do. Is it supposed to pack young people full of facts like a sausage, or is it supposed to niggle at them and kid them and irritate them just enough so they turn into pearls? Every sausage is alike. Every pearl is different. So let's take a look here at what this administration wants to turn into just another sausage."

The crowd didn't like being called a bunch of sausages, and the ones who were still listening stepped back a little. I worked my way closer, which meant stepping out into a wide-open space, a kind of no man's land between the uncommitted and the mostly committed. And where did I fit in? I started out wearing a white T-shirt and jeans but ended up wearing a vegetable. . . .

Just then, Larry untied Jordan's hands, tugging at the knot in the handkerchief. He waved for quiet. As if that was necessary.

Jordan reached for the buttons on her smock, undid them one by one: a weird striptease against censorship.

Then she slipped the last button free and stepped out of the loose nylon top. There was yesterday's dartboard bra. Blue, Rochelle, and Hector applauded and waved their fists

154

in the air. A few yards behind them, the signs went up and down.

"Now, this," Larry assured us, "is an art piece, pure and simple. Why? you ask. Because it can't be underwear. The darts would get in the way.

"Now as an art piece, I gotta admit I'm not sure what it's saying." He turned, put his arm around Jordan's shoulder, and said, "But we've got somebody here who is."

Jordan took the microphone with both hands. She waited until there was absolute silence, which didn't take long.

"You all know me," she said evenly. "Or at least you've seen me around and heard my big mouth. But when I really want to say something, I don't talk much. I make it with my hands.

"Last week I started to think about what it's like to be a girl today and how boys misunderstand and how most things—TV, ads, stuff like that—are on the boys' side.

"So I made this bra. These darts are the way some boys look at girls and the way that look hurts when it says, 'You're just a pair of boobs.'

"If you're a girl, those looks *are* like darts, and they stick in you all day. So if what I'm wearing will change one boy's mind, make one boy think twice before he starts drooling and acting out for his buddies, I'll be satisfied."

There was a little applause. Naturally from Blue and Hector and Rochelle, but from the kids with posters *and* from a few people standing among the Great Uncommitted.

Jordan leaned into the microphone. "The real question is, what am I doing up here all by myself?" She looked her audience over. Her eyes swept past me, darted back, swept on. "This isn't just for me. This isn't just so I can wear goofy clothes to school whenever I want. This is for you, too. All of you. So what am I doing up here all by myself?"

Everybody stirred, like a wind had blown through a garden.

"Let's say you stand there today and watch, and the school suspends me. Then you go back to class, right? Maybe you talk about it at lunch for a day or two or write an essay for English class. And then next month or next year you want to start a club or paint a sign or put on a play and somebody tells you, 'Sorry, it's vulgar' or 'It's disruptive' or 'It's too personal a statement.'

"Then what? Probably it's not too late. I admit that. You can have your own rally. You can call the ACLU. And do you know what they'll say? 'Sure, we can get your rights back, but it'd be easier if there was a precedent.' "

Jordan walked right to the edge of the stage. "I'm that precedent. So what am I doing up here all by myself?"

Nobody said anything. Everybody looked at the ground. Even Blue.

Then Ms. Christophe strolled from her place on the steps, made her way through the kids, climbed the three stairs. She reached for the microphone. Her other hand held a bunch of yellow referral slips.

"You're up here by yourself," she said, "because—"

It was now or never. "But she's not by herself!"

As I headed for the stage, everybody turned. I heard people ask, "Who's that?"

Ms. Christophe warned me. "Tony, you're looking at detention."

When I got closer, she said, "I'm warning you. One more step and it's Saturday school."

I vaulted up the stairs, glad there was a little railing because I sure needed something to hold on to. Everybody stared at me: Ms. Christophe, Larry, Jordan, the other kids. I mustered every bit of courage, unbuttoned my shirt, and let it fall.

"Just suspend me, too, and get it over with."

Everybody gaped at the two artichokes held onto my bare chest by twine and staples and duct tape. The laughter started, then built. A few kids clapping turned into a dozen, and that turned into a hundred.

"You should have told me!" shouted Blue. "I would've worn a couple of tubs of butter."

Ms. Christophe moaned, "Oh, my God."

Blue shouted. "And I'll show up tomorrow with a bra so big . . ."

"Me, too!" said Hector. "You'll have to suspend me, too."

Rochelle tore off her sweatshirt and began to fumble at the buttons of her blouse. "And me!"

Half the kids carrying posters stepped out and made their way toward us. I knew one girl's first name—Paula. She was pretty enough, smart enough, popular enough—what everybody means by "the average student." She walked right up beside Rochelle, put both hands on the top buttons of her Guess shirt, and shouted, "Me, too." Then her girlfriend stepped up and kids—mostly girls—started to run toward the stage from the back of the crowd.

Larry was shouting, "The number is 555-*LIPS*, that's 555–5477. I want you to call me!"

I stood there in my artichoke bra. My goose bumps. My red, embarrassed, happy face.

Larry Deluxe slapped me on the back. "Nice work," he bellowed.

"You did this for me!" Jordan said, slipping up beside me.

"Now do something for me." I reached for her. "Hold me up."

Epilogue

~~~~~

On the night of Art at the Mall, I drove the Subaru over to Jordan's house.

I glanced around. "Is she next door?"

Drew Archer shook his head. "At the mall since noon. Blue came by about four and picked up the tent. You know Jordan: everything's right down to the wire."

"But she'll finish this time?"

He took a big swallow of something right out of the blender. "Here's hoping," and he held up a set of crossed fingers.

"Maybe we should go see," I said, glancing at the clock. "It's almost seven-thirty."

Drew frowned. "The enzymes are best when they're fresh. Maybe I'll just take some along in a paper cup. You wouldn't mind, would you, Tony?"

"Well, I wouldn't want to damage my fabulous plastic upholstery, but since I promised Mom I wouldn't drive any faster than I can walk, I think it'll be okay."

As Drew locked the door, he looked around. "Where is your mother?"

"She had a job interview uptown; I dropped her off earlier. She said she'd meet us there."

"I thought she was working for Larry Deluxe."

"Well, until last week she was. If you call owing him five hundred dollars working."

"Owing him?"

"She flew to San Francisco with a firm offer of forty thousand a year and came back with a cool thirty-five. He was going to pay her ten percent, so she figures she owes him ten percent."

Drew Archer laughed. "He isn't going to take it, is he?"

I shook my head. "Probably just do a show on Women Who Owe Men Money."

Outside, I scrambled in my side of the car, leaned, and opened the door for him.

"You have to wear a seat belt, okay?" I reached into the glove compartment, handed him a folded piece of paper. "Check this out."

He read half out loud: " 'Driving contract: I, Tony Candelaria, do on this day agree to the stipulations stated below rendering me the privilege of driving my parent's car.' " He glanced over at me. "Jordan could use this for *Mementos of Totalitarianism*."

He read on. " 'Should I get a traffic ticket . . . at no time will I allow alcoholic beverages . . . seat belts . . . need for gas, oil, etcetera, etcetera.' Well, I feel very safe."

"Mom just said that she worried for fifteen years and she can't stop overnight. She almost didn't let me come get you because I'd be like three minutes without a licensed driver."

Drew watched me signal to change lanes on a deserted street, eye my rearview mirror, creep along at exactly thirty m.p.h.

"You're doing fine," he said, taking a huge pill.

159

We parked in the mall's lot and walked across the busy, one-way street. Drew reached into a coat pocket, took out a surgical mask, and slipped it over his mouth.

"There's some kind of flu going around."

"I figured."

"This should be interesting." Drew peered into big display windows full of boxy-looking fashions. "A juxtaposition of commerce and art."

"Have you seen this piece of hers?"

"No."

"I guess I'm wondering if I should borrow your mask or just put a bag over my head."

Drew Archer laughed as we stepped inside the big glass doors and looked the place over. Most of the main floor, at least the part you walk on, had been taken over: some paintings hung from wires like laundry, others from scatterboard that made walls with no rooms. Shoppers wove through those and the papier-mâché figures who writhed on the floor in front of The Limited.

"What's this one called?" Drew asked.

I checked the nearest white card. *"Angst."*

"I should have known." Then he pointed. "Aren't those your friends?"

I have to admit, that had a nice sound. "Yeah," I said.

Hector and Blue were circling an installation set up on industrial-strength rubber sheets. Different frozen organs—a heart, a liver, a something-or-other—were melting. The artist, wearing a butcher's apron over stiletto heels and fishnet stockings, stood nearby holding a sign—

Hazards of a Temperate Climate.

160

"Jordan's piece is a lot better than any of this stuff," Hector said. "Have you seen it?"

"Not yet."

"It's cool, man. Really." Then he waved. "Hang on a minute. I want you to meet my folks."

Hector's parents looked nervous. His mom kept tugging at the collar of her black dress and fanning herself. His dad was a big, strong-looking guy wearing a bolo tie.

"Are you an artist, too?" he asked, shaking my hand.

"No, sir."

He liked that. "Are you studying computers?"

"No, sir. I'm probably going to be a cook."

"Good for you!" He glared at his son. "People always have to eat. They don't always have to read comics."

Hector pretended to be mad. "Thanks, Tony. I owe you one."

Blue and I said good-bye. We made our way through shoppers with Shoe Time bags, we took in paintings of skeletons picking fruit glowing with pesticides, and of African American women nailed to crosses by white policemen.

"Where's yours?"

"I didn't finish. Thad got sick. Then Diane caught it." He shrugged. "What can I say." Blue stared at Saint Sebastian, riddled with toxic waste syringes, riding a surfboard at Malibu. "Jordan's a Michelangelo compared to these bozos."

"I sure hope so."

Mom and I spotted each other at the same time. "Did you get here all right?" she asked, nodding at Blue.

"Except for that crosswalk full of nuns."

She grinned at me. "You're a pretty good kid." She tried to fix my hair, which didn't need fixing, but I let her anyway.

"You're a pretty good mom."

"Really." She let her hand slide down one arm until she could squeeze my hand. "I'm sorry for everything, Tony."

"It wasn't your fault."

"No, not all of it." Then she took a deep breath and smiled. "By the way, I asked Sheila Larson for a job."

Automatically I looked for her black cowboy hat. "Sheila?"

"Tony, what do I know the most about?"

I was as good at making connections as the next high school student. But I still couldn't believe it. "Dead guys?"

"Exactly! And then we can stay here. For a while."

"Really?"

"I thought about what you said the other day. You were mad, but you were right, too. You've done a lot for me. It's my turn to do something for you."

"God, Mom. This is great. *You're* great."

She blushed. "It's been a long time since you said that."

"I'll tell you every day if you want."

She pushed me away, but she was just kidding around. Then she asked, "Did you see what Jordan did? Have you been inside? It's very creative! Very haunting somehow."

Just then Jordan slipped between some shoppers and headed toward us. She must have changed clothes because she had on new black jeans, and her blue cowboy shirt was pressed stiff. I could see that under it there was just a normal bra— no antlers or faucets. As she got closer, I felt Blue and my mom fade away.

"Did Dad come?" Jordan asked. "He heard on the radio that somebody in Oregon had a cold, so he wasn't sure he wanted to go out of the house."

"Over there. He's the one dressed like a surgeon."

She turned then. "Have you seen the piece yet?"

162

"No, uh . . ."

She pointed to a wide CONFESS-O-RAMA banner stretched over the entrance to a big black tent. "Go on. There's no line right now. And read the little sign on the outside." She pointed. "Just before you go in."

A white card said thanks to all the people who called in. Special thanks to Larry Deluxe for his assistance. Then at the bottom, on a line by itself—

THIS IS FOR TONY

I didn't turn around, I just hurried inside, then waited a few seconds to get my bearings. There were places like voting booths to step into and, at each station, headphones. Someone passed me on his way out, so I took his spot.

Straight ahead, right in front of me, a mirror was buried in the deep folds of black cloth so that we all stared into our own shadowy faces as we listened.

I picked up the warm headphones and slipped them on.

so lonely nobody understands how relentless my life is the life that can't be worth a thousand dollars for my husband doesn't remember the one who gets on everybody's nerves

That was my voice, the relentless part, the gets-on-everybody's-nerves part!

If my parents knew they'd think about boys all the time, too, the birth control pope said what the matter is how society lurks of course the police won't listen to some weird girl who's just different and the way men are crazy about looking at me dancing and dancing pretty well probably twenty hours a day by myself and really looking forward to it.

I took the headphones off. Wow. Dived back in.

more love than I could buy it's still pretty trying the housewife thing the right to be jealous in hindsight sure it's easy to look

163

back and criticize the mystery of how every desperate character
would be in this perfect little town the way things work out
though nothing ever not even with presoaking comes entirely
clean

A man's voice, then a woman's, a man again, an angry child, someone laughing—all sewn together.

So that's what she made out of what we'd all said, this moody, mysterious . . . I-don't-know-what that I was involved in.

I started to like finding my voice in it, the voice of a boy who was and wasn't me. Then I started to wonder that if I'd known how great this was going to be, would I have even been mad when I found out what she was up to? Would I have wanted her to stop me from calling, after all? In a way I was glad to be part of this—out there with everybody else.

I listened some more—it got better the second time—and then I stepped outside where Jordan was waiting, fidgeting a little, staring into space. Behind her I heard Larry's good-natured laugh, I could see Hector, and now Rochelle. There were the puzzled shoppers; the kids clustered around one another; my mom wearing Sheila Larson's black hat.

Jordan spotted me, took a step forward, then one back.

I walked straight to her, grinning, holding out both arms.

"Yes!" She sounded like I'd scored the winning touchdown. She put one hand to her chest. "I didn't know what I was going to do if you hadn't . . ."

"Don't worry about that. It's great. Really."

"I couldn't have finished this without you. Not just the things you said on the tape; I had plenty of those. But the way you held me together when I got weird and how you came to the rally and school and . . ."

"It turned out great."

164

I heard my mother laugh, then saw her lean into Sheila and laugh some more.

I looked over my shoulder at Jordan's creation. "C'mon. *Confess-O-Rama*'s almost empty right now. And it's dark in there. Let's go in and listen together."